MONOGAMY WITH TREATS

MONOGAMY
WITH
TREATS

VOL. 1

PEEKABOO COLLINS

Monogamy With Treats Vol. 1

ISBN: 197921347X
ISBN-13: 978-1979213479

Printed in the United States of America

For any typos in or inquiries regarding this book, please email:
pika@monogamywithtreats.com

for the Peekaboo Collins in all of us:
the free thinkers, truth seekers, and risk takers – this one's for you.

Episodes

Introduction

This book is a journey into the minds of lovers. Written from the perspectives of various couples, these stories are about having the courage to explore one's deepest desires, as well as the lengths to which two people in love will go in order to fulfill each other's every desire.

The couples in these stories are exemplary of the notion that with true, unconditional love, two people who are living in their truth and caring for each other selflessly can develop a relationship that is fun, satisfying, and pleasurable. The effort the characters put into loving their partners and caring for the "treats" they encounter sets the stage for the deep connections they develop.

I hope to transport you into another world to show you everything you want in a relationship is possible if you're willing to put in the work it takes to achieve it. I am writing to the Peekaboo Collins in all of us. I write to find you, because just by picking up this book, you have already found me.

I write to bring you into my world, my fantasyland, to bring you inside the experiences of the characters in each story, to put you inside the situations. I write to inspire you, to help you see beyond societal norms, and to urge you to join in the quest for liberty of expression.

   Monogamy with Treats Vol.1 is just the beginning of the journey, the first book in the MWT series. I hope these stories will empower you and inspire you, or at the very least, turn you on—not just between your legs, but between your ears and in your heart, as well. Cheers!

Slippery When Wet

Lena

I moved to New York City six months ago for an amazing job opportunity, and I couldn't have been more excited. Although I didn't know anyone in the city when I first moved, I became fast friends with my new roommate, Miles, and I was eager to make new connections.

One weekend, Miles invited me out to a birthday party for a new friend of his and I agreed to go, even though I'd know no one there. We were extremely early, so we decided to check out another spot for a drink or two to kill time.

I got dressed to the nines, as always, and we headed out. A friend of his I had met once or twice was at the bar waiting for us, also early. As the only female in our trio, I decided to venture off on my own to check out the scene. I didn't want to limit myself by appearing to be with a boyfriend, and being almost six feet tall in heels, I didn't want to intimidate any women who might have been interested in my guys.

It wasn't long before I caught the eye of a particularly attractive gentleman who stood at least six inches taller than me. He stepped to me with his best pickup line.

"How do you feel about older men?" he asked.

I paused a beat, considering how to answer this absurd attempt at flirtation.

"I don't really feel any way about older men. If you're asking if I have a problem dating them, then no, I don't." I searched for signs of age, but came up short. "My dad is seventeen years older than my mom, so it's kind of the norm for me."

His full lips curled into a smirk that suggested satisfaction. "So have you followed in her footsteps?"

"No," I blurted out, more aggressively than intended. "I mean, I just never have."

"Would it scare you?"

I thought to myself, "Scare me? Honestly, considering how immature guys my own age are, perhaps an older man is just what I need." I brushed those thoughts aside, as I was enjoying being single in this big city and liked the freedom I had to explore whatever, and whoever, came my way.

I looked up at him and shook my head without saying a word. He must have realized that his question distracted me by the look on my face. He changed the subject, not knowing what I was thinking and not willing to risk ending the conversation.

He leaned down so he didn't have to speak over the old-school hip-hop music bumping through the speakers. "My name is Jay."

"I'm Lena."

"It's nice to meet you, Lena. So who are you here with?"

I pulled away from him slightly so that he could see my face. "I came with my roommate and we met his friend here."

I was curious to see how this guy would react to the gender-specific pronoun I used in describing my roommate. Not a single eyebrow lifted. I looked back over my shoulder. "Those two over there," I said as I nodded in their direction.

"How about you invite them over for a drink – I have a tab open at the bar you're welcome to drink on."

"I'll go over and ask them, I'll be right back." I turned to leave.

Miles and his friend were expectedly unenthused at the idea of drinking on another man's tab. I, however, was all too sober for my own liking, and with time to kill before we headed to the next spot, I decided to accept his invitation.

"There she is." Jay smiled at me as I walked toward where he stood at the bar.

"No luck." I smiled back.

"No worries. What would you like to drink?"

"Tequila on the rocks. I don't have a preference."

Jay reached out and around me, putting his hand on the small of my back, pulling me closer to him as he leaned toward the bartender. She handed me my drink as Jay faced me, removing his hand from my waist.

"I told myself I wasn't going to hit on you, but I just had to tell you how beautiful you are. From the moment I noticed you walk in."

"Well, thank you," I said confidently.

"So Lena, what do you do in the city?" he asked.

"I just moved here six months ago; I work in marketing. And you?"

He nodded with interest. "Marketing ... nice. I used to play in the NBA but I'm retired. Now I work in real estate."

I looked at him skeptically. I recognized neither his face nor his name, and simply didn't believe him.

He smiled broadly. "What's that face for?"

I forgot how effortlessly, and often carelessly, I wore my emotions all over my face.

"What team did you play for?" I asked suspiciously.

"The Nets back when they were in Jersey. I'm aging myself again, but it might have been before your time."

I thought to myself, "Ah, a likely reason I have no clue who you are."

As timing would have it, a friend of Jay's came over to join the conversation. I made a mental note to pay attention to how people treated this guy. He did have a certain swag about him ...

I excused myself to order another drink, not needing to mention to the bartender the name of the tab. She winked at me as if she knew a dirty little secret before walking away. My curiosity was officially piqued.

Just then, I saw Miles out of the corner of my eye. It looked as if he had been trying to make eye contact with me, and I could see his relief. It was time to go.

Jay was deep in conversation with his friend at this point, so I wrote my name and number on a bar napkin and left it with another of his friends before giving Jay a quick wave goodbye. He made a face as if to apologize. I smiled back at him reassuringly before heading for the door, placing my empty glass on the end of the bar. As I turned to leave, a hand grabbed my arm gently and I spun around to see Jay standing in front of me.

"Sorry about that, I could barely pull myself away," he feigned annoyance. "I know you have to leave, but I wanted to thank you for joining me. It was a pleasure meeting you."

"It was nice to meet you, too. And thanks for the drinks … I left my number with your friend. Hopefully you can get it from him without him thinking I meant it to be for him." I winked and smiled at him.

"Goodnight, Jay," I added as I turned to leave.

He smiled back. "Goodnight, Lena. Be safe."

Monday morning, as I was telling my co-worker Matt all about my weekend, I finally heard from Jay. I let the unfamiliar number go to voicemail. Right after the voicemail alert, I got a text message:

> Hey Lena, it's Jay. I left you a voicemail but in case you didn't recognize the number, I want to tell you again how much I enjoyed meeting you on Friday. Hopefully we can keep in touch and you'll let me take you out soon.

My pussy throbbed as I read that this man wanted to see me again. After not hearing from him over the weekend, I hadn't been sure if I'd ever hear from him again.

"Wait, you said this dude played in the NBA back in the day?" Matt asked, interrupting my thoughts. "What's his name? I might know him."

"Yeah, for the New Jersey Nets. His name is Jay. He didn't mention a last name."

A minute or so later, while I was busy reading and rereading this text message, Matt popped up from over his cubicle. "Got him! Yeah, I know this dude. He wasn't an All-Star or anything but I remember him from back in the day. Are you gonna go out with him?"

"I don't know." I shrugged. "Pro ballers aren't really my thing. They're usually players, and I'm not in the mood to be played."

Matt and I spent the next ten or so minutes looking at highlight clips of Jay. Although I generally did not like the idea of getting involved with professional athletes, my pussy was disagreeing with me. I could feel myself getting wetter and wetter, not because this guy played pro, but because out of all the girls in the bar that night, he wanted me. Now he wanted more of me.

"Oh, come on, Lena," Matt teased. "At least let him take you out for dinner, just to say you did it. What's the problem?"

"The problem is I just moved here not even a year ago and I'm enjoying myself. An older, well-established guy is most likely looking for something serious."

"Will you just do it, Lena, and stop being such a pussy?" Matt insisted. "It's just one date."

"I'll think about it." I rolled my eyes at him hanging over the wall that separated our desks. "But I'll tell you one thing—I'm not going to sleep with him," I promised, more to myself than to Matt. "I'm doing things differently this time. This man looked at me like if I gave him some pussy he'd chew right through me. No ... this one's gonna wait. I don't care if he played ball, he's gonna have to earn it." I was sick and tired of these guys who just wanted to waste my time to get a piece of ass.

The very example of the standard I was used to was only a few desks away from me. Luke was physically my exact type and could talk the panties off a lesbian. The way he looked at me as he walked by my desk made me swoon every time. He and Matt were good friends, having both been with the company much longer than me, so Luke often used Matt as an excuse to come over and chat. He had such a gift of gab that he could flirt with me without Matt even realizing it, but it was no secret that Luke and I had been spending time together outside of work. It was hard to deny someone who was in my face every day talking that smooth talk, but it didn't take long for me to figure out that his intentions didn't go past the bedroom.

To my great misfortune, behind closed doors, this man could not walk the walk and keep his dick hard. At first I thought it was something I was doing wrong, but after every time we slept together, he would continue to pursue me at work and make more promises for the bedroom that he couldn't keep. I hated the fact that I was so attracted to someone who was otherwise such a disappointment, but I kept going back because he didn't have any competition, and it became my goal to conquer him. I became addicted to a certain kind of power in making this smooth talker buckle at the knees.

But my pussy was craving a grown man to take care of her the right way, and she already had her lips set on Jay. Just the thought of his big hands and his muscular arms had me in the bathroom at work playing with myself, imagining his dick deep inside my juicy pussy. Knowing I'd be making this man I craved so badly wait, not even sure I'd ever sleep with him, I hoped Luke would finally start acting the way he talked.

"Maybe if we tried something new, fucking in public or something, he'd be able to fuck me the way I wish he would," I thought.

"Fat chance," my pussy reminded me.

Jay

I was finally able to convince my friend to give me Lena's number after his failed attempts to get in touch with her over the weekend. He was my boy, but he wasn't exactly skilled with the ladies, not knowing it was best to leave a voicemail if he was going to be calling someone he just met. I was pleased, however, because he was able to see the number was intended for me, and eventually handed it over. I had been occupied for most of the night entertaining out-of-town friends, and so I wasn't sure if Lena would respond. Regardless, I had to try.

In all my years playing ball and being on the road, I had never met a more beautiful woman. She was clearly younger than me, but even in the few lines we exchanged, she had an old-school vibe to her and a wittiness that playfully forced my full attention She was beautiful on the outside, too; long, curly brown hair, piercing blue eyes, and long, toned legs. Her energy was undeniable, and an inexplicable longing to have her consumed me.

I called her Monday morning, and after leaving a voicemail I decided to text her as well so she would know it was me. She didn't respond right away, and I couldn't stop thinking about her until she did, some hours later. I invited her to dinner on Friday, which she agreed to, nonchalantly. Her no-bullshit attitude turned me on. I knew she would be different from anyone I had ever known. Even years after retiring from the NBA, women still lost their senses and ended up acting more useful as a doormat than a partner when I gave them a chance. Lena hardly seemed bothered, which made me want to bring my A-game.

On Thursday afternoon, I couldn't get Lena off my mind, so I invited her to grab a drink with me when she got off work. She was concerned I was cancelling our date the next day, which I assured her I wasn't; I just couldn't wait to see her. She was not the type of woman to trade a dinner date for drinks. She agreed under the condition we would still do dinner the next night and met me after work that evening.

Drinks on Thursday and dinner on Friday turned into five days straight of us hitting all of the city's hotspots.

She was insatiable, never before having experienced the city at the level I showed her that weekend. The funny part was, Lena made it clear up front I wouldn't be getting pussy from her anytime soon. She wanted us to get to know each other first.

Little did she know, I fell in love with everything about her that weekend. Her sexy laugh, the way she carried herself, those light eyes, her hard protruding nipples that showed through the silky shirts she wore on our dates. How badly I wanted to suck on them and squeeze them. She commanded the attention of every room she entered with her confidence and made me feel like for once, I was not the celebrity.

My brain was on board with taking the time to make her mine, but my dick never failed to remind me how painful a journey it would be until she finally allowed me to feel how tight that pussy was.

A month after we started dating, I asked to see her outside of the city. I had an office in Miami and was down for the weekend, and I thought it would be the perfect chance to switch up our dating scene. I wanted to see if this chick could hang as well on South Beach as she could in the Big Apple.

I grabbed my phone. It was midday, so surely Lena was at work. I opened up my messages.

> Hey beautiful. I'm sure you're at work right now, but what do you say I book you a flight to come meet me in Miami this weekend?

A few minutes passed before my phone beeped.

> Hmm... that sounds nice. Are you being serious?

> Yeah, I miss you

> I have a few meetings at the end of the week but I thought if you wanted to come down I'd extend my trip a couple days.

> I'd like that. But I do want to make a few things clear before I agree...

I shook my head and smiled. "Here we go," I said aloud to the empty room; my words figuratively rolled their eyes as they escaped my lips.

> You've been very respectful, and I thank you for that. I just want to make it clear that there are no expectations of us sleeping together just because I'm allowing you to fly me to another city.

I knew that one was coming. What I didn't expect was the level of admiration I felt reading that text. Lena always spoke her mind, and made her own boundaries clear. She was certainly a woman that knew what she wanted, and didn't want, and was never afraid to say it.

Lena still hadn't yet given up the pussy, and although I was dying to fuck her, I learned not to expect that to happen. Things were going great between us and I wasn't about to fuck it up by trying to make a move on her. She had told me when she was ready she'd make it very clear.

> You have my word.

> When you have a minute, let me know when's a good time for you to fly out and I'll book it. You don't mind if we share a bed, do you?

> Very funny, smartass. You're a bed hog and you snore, so as long as it's at least a queen, I think I can manage 😩😩

This time it was my eyes that rolled. We had spent the night with each other only a handful of times, and every time she not only ended up with all the blankets, but more times than not I had to wake her up so that I wouldn't fall off the bed.

> Lies, all lies 😵 😵 😖 but you got it. Just wanted to make sure up front. As always, your lead. You're worth the wait, Lena. Let me know about the flight.

> I was planning on working a half day Friday, so any time after 4pm is fine. Newark or LGA, either works.

There went that signature Lena nonchalance. I smiled again. Many other women would have lost it at the invitation for an all-expenses-paid-for weekend getaway, yet here was Lena barely blinking a digital eye. Man, I wanted this chick. Bad.

Barely forty-eight hours later she was walking off the plane, ready for fun in her flowing sundress. I had reserved a nice hotel on the beach around the best shops in case this weekend together would be more out and about than suckin' and fuckin'. "Her lead," I reminded myself.

We checked into the hotel and got settled, then went to dinner on the beach to catch up. As soon as the waitress took our order, Lena dove right into conversation.

"How come you always leave town so abruptly after we spend a lot of time together?" She raised an eyebrow, eyeing me skeptically.

I made sure to choose my words wisely. "I figured that perhaps you like your space. I've never asked why you haven't allowed us to be very physical yet; I just figured you're dating other people."

"There's this one guy, Luke. Despite having promised my mother otherwise before I moved to New York, I work with him." She shrugged unapologetically but her expression revealed faint remorse.

I sat and listened intently, not wanting to interrupt her opening up about something this personal for the first time.

"He's pretty pathetic, if I'm going to be honest," she stated matter-of-factly before bursting into a fit of giggles. "I truly didn't want to sleep with someone I work with, but he challenged me, and I'm attracted, so I went for it," she admitted, looking directly at me.

"Challenged you how?"

"Always talking about how I wouldn't be able to handle it … how I must be scared … blah blah blah. I wanted to show him he ain't shit, so I did." She snickered. "Turns out *he*'s the one who can't handle *me*." She shrugged and continued.

"Sure I'm attracted to him, but I had never slept with someone just to shut them up before. Unfortunately, it didn't shut him up." Lena rolled her eyes. "I see him differently, though, and he doesn't have as much of an effect on me, which is nice. I'm sure my boss likes it, too; I'm much more productive now." Another fit of giggles shook through her.

I enjoyed watching how much Lena glowed in her truth.

"It seems as though you're content in your decision to sleep with him, even though he sounds like a punk," I teased, wanting to keep the conversation progressing, yet comfortable.

"He's a punk, alright." She shook her head. "But yeah, I don't regret it. I do wish he could have been a bit more worth it, though."

"What do you mean 'worth it'? You had to have known that a guy who talks so much probably feels the need to do so for a reason, right?"

"I guess I was caught up in my flesh. He seemed so confident, so certain, and he just ended up being *so* unsatisfying ..." she trailed off.

"You like the freedom of being single, don't you? Able to make your own decisions?"

"I do. But I'm slowly leaning toward wanting something else. It scares me a little bit how much I like spending time with you. It's why I secretly enjoy that you travel so much," she admitted.

I was excited at her honesty. "Baby, if you truly want to be treated how you deserve, I would be more than honored to show you. You're worth far more than these guys you're filling your time with."

I leaned in close to her and kissed her neck. She immediately melted at my touch and tilted her head to allow me easier access. I nibbled on her earlobe as she moaned softly. Crumbling her walls had become one of my favorite feats.

"I can show you depths of yourself you have never experienced, from the inside out." I kissed behind her ear. "Whenever you're ready, I'll show that pussy exactly how a grown man should handle her," I whispered.

She moaned deeper and pulled away, looking directly into my eyes, as if searching them, our faces inches apart. She leaned in and drove her tongue into my mouth. Our tongues danced around each other's with a passion we had not yet reached. I felt a deep yearning from Lena for the very first time. I wanted to take full advantage of this breakthrough.

"Tell me, Lena, what scares you about how much you enjoy our time together? What are you so afraid of?"

She tilted her head so that her mouth was against my ear. "Becoming too attached to someone who ends up letting me down."

"That's why you fucked Luke. A part of you knew he would let you down. You didn't have to worry about becoming attached, am I right?"

She shifted in her seat.

"You're right," she affirmed.

"You also know that once you allow me to treat you the way you should be treated, that feeling of wanting something else will become more intense, don't you? Is that what you're afraid of?"

"Yeah," she breathed. I kissed her again.

It all began to make sense.

"And you're afraid of losing your independence, because that's what happened in all your other relationships, right?"

She paused. "Yes."

I pulled away from her slightly and took her face in my hands. "Will you allow me to show you that you have nothing to be afraid of?"

She nodded her head.

"Will you allow me to show you how you deserve to be treated without you having to sacrifice who you are?"

The pressure in her shoulders visibly fled her body. She nodded again.

"And will you allow me to take care of that pussy how she deserves to be taken care of when you're ready?"

She smiled a wide smile. "My lead," she promised, and kissed me again.

Just then, the waitress came with our food. We hadn't noticed that she had brought us our drinks already, the condensation noticeable on the glasses. I thanked the waitress and turned back toward Lena, sucking gently on her neck one last time. "You better eat quickly, we're not done with this conversation."

Lena smiled a playful smile. "My lead," she teased, as I pinched her leg above the knee, causing her to jump and fall into another fit of giggles. I couldn't get enough of her.

We ate, making lighter talk between bites. I asked her how her most recent project was going at work, and we talked about how business was going for me, until Lena dove right in again.

"Do you like to be dominant in the bedroom?" she blurted out.

It was a good thing I was sitting down, as my dick began to swell at her question. For someone who was rather standoffish with me physically, her smallest offerings commanded my full attention.

"That depends on how you define dominant. I like to take care of my woman, however that means for her."

"When I'm ready, I want you to dominate me, whatever that means to you." She smirked playfully. "I don't want a second to pass that I'm not reminded I'm dealing with a grown man."

"A real man takes his time. You just have to guide me. Your lead, as you always say."

"It's only my lead until we get to where we're going, then I want you to take over. Then it's your lead."

"You got it, baby."

"I'll let you know if you're going too fast, or too far."

I wasn't sure if she was talking about the near or far future, but I didn't doubt for a second that she was getting closer to allowing me to find out.

Suddenly, I had an idea.

Lena

We finished dinner and Jay suggested we hit the strip club. After all the naughty talk, I was feeling closer to him than ever. I had never been to a strip club but I was excited to finally explore the sexier side of a relationship with Jay.

We went back to the hotel to freshen up and Jay popped a bottle of champagne. He poured us each a coffee cup the room provided and made a toast.

"To our first weekend together away from the big city, and our first of many weekend getaways," he said. We touched cups.

It was still too early for the strip club, so we hung out in the room and finished the champagne. Jay could tell I was getting antsy, so he suggested we get to it. I grabbed my clutch and we hopped into the rental car.

We entered the club to find half-naked women of all shapes and shades everywhere. We were shown to a table, then a cute brunette waitress came over to take our order.

"Two rum and Cokes," Jay told her without hesitation. His attention to detail made my pussy throb.

The waitress came back a few minutes later. While Jay was busy setting up a tab with her, a curvy but petite dancer with a bright pink G-string bikini and perfect tits came over and sat on my lap. She introduced herself as "B."

I always knew I was somewhat into women, but I had never experienced one before. I had never even felt a pair of tits besides my own! B smelled so sweet. Her skin was like silk under my fingertips. She slowly rubbed her ass in small circles on my lap while I ran my fingers up and down her back.

I looked over at Jay, who was watching us as he smiled at me and gave me a nod of encouragement. This chick on my lap was so delicious. I wanted to see if Jay was really comfortable with me giving all my attention to someone else. Although he mentioned at dinner that he knew I was dating other people and that he wanted to be the one to show me how this pussy deserved to be treated, I had to challenge that and see how he would react. After all the empty shit-talking that Luke did, I needed to make sure Jay was sincere.

Being a rookie to the strip club scene, I had no idea how much I was allowed to touch the girls. B figured out right away I didn't really know what I was doing and took my hands to direct them all over her thick thighs, her ass, and her amazing tits. With her hand on top of mine, she traced over her every curve, allowing me to feel all over her. I could not believe how much I enjoyed touching another woman and before I knew it I was playing with her pussy over her G-string. She was grinding on me and feeling herself all over as I rubbed her clit, feeling it swell under my fingers.

Jay watched the whole thing and even talked away the bouncer when he came over to make sure B was not in a disagreeable situation. Jay did everything he could to protect us and to allow me to continue to enjoy myself. My pussy was soaking wet not only from B, but also from the mere thought that Jay really cared about my pleasure and enjoyment.

On the ride back to the hotel, Jay could not stop smiling.

"Have you ever been with a woman?" he asked me.

"No ... but I've always been attracted to them. You just witnessed the most I've ever done." I shot him an evocative glance.

"It was so hot to watch you explore her. Could you see yourself being with a female?"

I was silent for a few moments, thinking to myself.

Shyly, I admitted, "I used to say I could never be with a girl ... maybe let her go down on me. But after tonight ... and B ... I think I could. I was so fucking into her."

What I wanted to say was that as long as Jay was in the room, I would be down for trying anything. My pussy throbbed in agreement, but I kept that thought to myself, not wanting to give Jay any premature ideas.

"Did you enjoy watching me with B?" I asked.

"Hell yeah. Honestly, I've never enjoyed watching a girl I'm dating enjoying herself with someone else more. It turns me on to see you pleased, if that makes sense ..."

I realized then why Jay suggested we go to the strip club. He wanted to see what my limits were, and where my boundaries lay. He was turned on not because he was watching two chicks damn near finger-fucking each other, but because he realized the possibilities that came along with dating me. I was wildly turned on sitting there in the car thinking about how this man's brain worked.

It was the first time I ever felt like someone cared more about my pleasure than his own. For once it wasn't all about the guy, but about me. My pussy was throbbing, begging me to allow Jay to fulfill his promise to take care of her. And it was about damn time. But first, I wanted to show this man that although B was hot as hell, he was the one I wanted to please.

Jay

We got back to the hotel and Lena told me to sit in the chair in the corner. She poured us both a drink and made her way to the bathroom. When she emerged, she had nothing on but the red-bottomed heels she wore to the strip club. Her body was completely hairless and her skin looked like butter. It was the first time I had seen her completely naked, and despite our talk over dinner, I reminded myself to keep my expectations low.

Lena walked over to the USB dock near the bed, plugged in her iPhone and turned on some sultry music. She turned around to face me, maintaining eye contact with me as she walked slowly toward me. She danced around me, swaying her hips back and forth while she rubbed on her tits. It seemed as though my idea of the strip club had inspired Lena to show me those girls had nothing on her. I sat there enjoying the show, smiling to myself at the fact that even with all her clothes on, Lena turned me on far more than any of them. Regardless, B was worth every dollar.

As Lena danced, she got closer and closer to me until she was right in front of me. She turned around slowly and spread her legs, and then bent over, her pussy lips wide open in front of my face. I reached out and ran my hand up the outside of her thigh, expecting her to stop me at any moment. She stood there bent over, swaying back and forth ever so slightly to the beat, allowing my hand to travel up her thigh and onto her ass. I took my other hand and put both of them on her cheeks, grabbing them gently.

I sat up straight and leaned forward so her ass was right in my face as I continued to rub all over her. Her pussy juice slowly dripped down her inner thigh. Daringly, I slid my hand in between her legs and with my thumb, rubbed her wetness back up toward her pussy. I let my thumb run along her pussy lips up toward her ass. She was so wet. Her entire pussy glistened in front of my face.

I so badly wanted to taste her but I didn't want to ruin the moment. Instead, I slowly moved my thumb back down between her pussy lips and back up again. After a few times, I turned my hand palm up and ran my whole hand over her pussy, her juices all over me.

I slowly stuck one finger, and then two fingers inside of her until she let me play with her pussy in my hands any way I wanted. We had arrived.

"My lead," I commanded.

"Your lead, baby," she confirmed.

As I was fucking her with my fingers, she sat down backward on my lap, spreading her pussy even wider for my enjoyment. Her hips spread over my legs and she gyrated her ass on my lap, my hand the only thing keeping her wetness from making a mess on me. With my other hand, I reached around and grabbed her gently by the neck as I continued to play with her pussy. Suddenly, she leaned backward so her back was against me, her tits up in the air and my hand still around her neck. I slid my hand down her chest.

She kicked her heels off and one at a time, got her legs out from under her and sat up directly on my lap for balance. With one hand on my thigh, she reached under herself with her other hand and slowly removed my fingers from inside her. She stood up, turned around and faced me, and extended her hand to me. I took it and she pulled me to my feet and began unbuttoning my shirt, staring into my eyes. She removed my shirt and undid my belt, but I wasn't finished with her yet.

Lena

As much as I was enjoying the finger assault on my pussy, the rest of this evening was supposed to be about pleasing Jay. Although he had made it clear in the car that my pleasure brought him the most happiness of all, I still wanted to take care of him. I had made him wait long enough and now I needed him to know how badly I wanted him.

I took his shirt off and ran my fingers down his chest, over his chiseled abs, and stopped at his waist. As I undid his belt with one hand, he grabbed me by the shoulders, spun me around, and pushed me up against the wall. My pussy cheered with applause, at last allowed to be the star of the show. She was finally getting the attention she deserved. She throbbed at the rough way Jay was handling me and I silently thanked myself for making this man wait so long. My pussy rolled her eyes.

Jay reached underneath me and spread my legs further apart before he grabbed my neck once more. He rubbed all over my ass with his other hand, giving one cheek a hard smack. The sting was immediate as he quickly rubbed hard right where his hand made contact to soothe my aching flesh. As the sting was subsiding, he gave me another hard smack, rubbing the pain again while holding me still with his other hand around my neck. No one had ever used such force with me, and it turned me on so much for a man to take control for once.

I moaned audibly, "Don't stop."

As he rubbed the pain from his second slap, he brought his face close to my ear and whispered, "My lead, right?"

At this point, I was ready to submit to anything this man asked of me. He had obeyed my wishes of taking his time with me, and it was about time I got out of my own damn way and let this man have his naughty way with me.

"Your lead," I managed to say with my face still against the wall.

He spun me around to face him. "Do you trust me?" he asked, looking directly into my eyes. "Remember, if it's too much—"

"I trust you, Jay." I interrupted him. "I remember what I said." He took my face in both hands, pressed his body into mine and kissed me.

After about a minute, he pulled away and with a smile, said, "Good," before spinning me around again to face the wall. With his hand he rubbed my juices all over my anus as he worked his fingers slowly inside. First one finger, and then a second finger entered my ass. This man was clearly here to claim every inch of me, and damn it felt so good.

As he fucked my ass with his fingers, my pussy gushed beneath me. I lost my breath as he reached around and played with my clit at the same time. All I could do was arch my back and hold on to the wall in attempt to balance. The only thing truly keeping me on my feet was Jay's hands underneath me. Just then, he removed his fingers from my ass and gave me a third hard slap, this time letting the sting linger as I felt a cold sensation near my anus.

It was the champagne bottle we shared after dinner before hitting the strip club. He grabbed me around the hip with the hand that had just been in my pussy, and slowly worked the champagne bottle into my ass neck first. The pressure was the most amazing sensation I had ever felt. The wetness from my pussy allowed the champagne bottle to slide in and out of my ass with ease and I could barely stay on my feet.

What possessed me to allow this man to continue fucking my ass with a champagne bottle I had no idea, but it felt so damn good and after all, it was Jay's big hand holding the other end. He worked the bottle deeper into my ass, spreading it wide open. All I could think about was how badly I couldn't wait until that champagne bottle was replaced by Jay's hard dick.

I thought, "What is it about this man that makes me want to do everything and anything with him?"

All of a sudden, Jay removed the bottle from my ass, whisked me off my feet and threw me onto the bed. Clearly this man had no intention of allowing me to please him, but I could tell after weeks of waiting, he was excited to finally have me. Jay crawled on top of me, his pants still on, and we kissed for a long time. I wrapped my legs around him and cradled his face in both my hands. He then moved down to my neck and kissed me everywhere his hand had been not moments before.

The care he took in pleasing me was like nothing I had ever experienced. He kissed down my breasts, and further to my stomach. He kissed both of my inner thighs and then stopped and looked up at me between my legs. I smiled at him and nodded, giving him permission to taste me for the first time. Instead of going down on me like I thought he would, he came all the way back up to meet my face with his. He had an expression I had never seen on him before. It was serious, and it concerned me a bit.

"Lena, I've loved you since our third date and I want you to be mine. I've been waiting patiently to give you the world and I want you to finally allow me to give it to you, if you will."

I couldn't move. I stared at him and knew he was serious. Deep down I had already loved him for a while now, too.

"My heart has belonged to you for some time now," I admitted.

With those words, he kissed me again. "I love you, Lena. Now I want to taste what's mine."

Before I could say anything more, he kissed his way back down my body. I gasped with each connection his mouth made to my skin. From head to toe, I was covered in goosebumps.

I held the sides of his head as he made his way down, my pussy throbbing uncontrollably from his admission that he loved me and the silent celebration she was doing from my allowance of finally agreeing to be treated the way we both deserved.

This time he went straight for my clit. The sensation of his tongue knowing exactly where to focus was almost enough to send me over the edge. I was still soaking wet from the past hour or so and he licked it all up, taking his time not to make me cum before he got his fill. I arched my back and wrapped my legs around his shoulders as he grabbed and massaged my ass underneath me. I squeezed my pussy walls tight each time he swirled his tongue around my clit, bringing me closer and closer to climax. As my moans quickened and he realized I was getting close, he stuck one finger inside my pussy and relentlessly massaged my G-spot as his tongue went crazy on my clit. The sensation together was more than I could stand and I screamed out, "Jay, I'm gonna cum! Oh my god, baby, I'm cumming!"

He didn't stop with his tongue until my body was convulsing and I desperately pushed his head away from my pussy, so sensitive I couldn't stand another lick. Jay kissed his way back up to my lips and tongue kissed me deeply, allowing me to taste what was now his.

I must have fallen asleep. When I woke up, it was light out, and I panicked, embarrassed.

"How could I have fallen asleep on him?" I thought to myself, annoyed. "So much for taking care of him last night." I rolled my eyes at myself as my pussy throbbed in utter satisfaction. "Selfish bitch."

I looked over at Jay sleeping next to me. He still had his pants on, which led me to believe he didn't even try to fuck me last night. Could this man get any more perfect? Here I was stark naked, having just committed myself to this man, and he didn't try to use that to his advantage?

Immediately, my pussy began to throb for a different reason: I needed to have this man inside me. I needed him to take this pussy like he promised. I needed him to make this pussy his, once and for all. I stirred, hoping that rubbing my skin against him would wake him, but to no avail.

I could not tolerate another second without him inside me. I put my hand on his shoulder and turned him onto his back. He slowly came to as I massaged his dick to get it hard.

"What's up, baby? You okay?" he asked me.

I was far from okay.

"I want you inside me, baby. I need you inside me. I can't wait another minute longer."

He immediately woke. His dick grew super hard in my hand. He undid his belt and let down his zipper before sliding his pants off. His dick was rock hard and stood straight up in the air. It was bigger than I could have ever imagined; my pussy did a double backflip. Jay reached over to the nightstand and grabbed a condom, sliding it on in no time at all. He pushed me onto my back and got on top of me.

"Lena, I have been waiting for you to submit to me and I am honored to have all of you. I love you, Lena." Once again, before I could say anything, he slammed his hard dick all the way inside me so deep that I lost my breath. Jay took his time with me, giving me long, deep strokes, making every inch of my pussy his and letting me know the Lukes of the world were in the past and that he was here to stay.

Jay

Despite having been awakened from a deep sleep, it was go time. Finally feeling the deliciousness of this pussy I just made mine, I wanted to get even deeper and hit every single inch of it. I grabbed both of Lena's legs, one at a time, and put them over my shoulders as I sat up, going even deeper into her gushing pussy. I played with her clit as I held one leg in place with my other hand. She opened her other leg to the side, spreading her pussy wide open, giving me a courtside seat to her perfect, pink little pussy. I watched her lips spread open around me as I dug deep inside her, her lips hugging my dick tightly as I pulled out, over and over. It was as if her pussy was talking to me, reacting internally with every stroke. I had never felt a pussy so wet in my life and it got wetter and wetter the more I made love to it. Her idea to get to know each other before getting physical proved to be worth it. Her pussy ached for me.

Suddenly a thought crossed my mind and I pulled out of her. "Come here, I have an idea." I got off the bed and went to the bathroom to get two towels. I came back to the bed and held out my hand to help Lena up. As soon as she was standing I handed her a towel.

"Wrap this around yourself and come with me," I commanded, as I headed for the sliding glass doors that led directly to the pool. I wrapped my towel around my waist just before I got to the door.

Hesitantly, Lena followed my lead, ass naked aside from the little towel covering her tall, slender frame. She looked disappointed.

"Baby, where are we going?" she asked. I was already by the pool, leaving her no choice but to follow me outside. A few people were sunbathing. I looked back to make sure Lena was behind me and saw the realization of my intentions hit her. I gave her a sly smile.

She ran up behind me and grabbed my arm. "Baby, NO!" she pleaded in a hushed voice.

"Do you trust me?" There was that question again.

"Of course I do, but this is crazy."

"Shh, just trust me. Come here." I took her hand off my arm and led her around to the stairs. We both walked into the pool with our towels on and I pulled Lena to the deep end, as far away from everyone as possible.

I pushed her against the edge of the pool, wrapped her legs around my waist and slid right back inside her slippery pussy. She gasped, surprised at how easily I was able to enter her despite the water washing away some of her wetness. She looked around nervously as our rhythm created ripples on the surface of the water.

"Baby, relax, no one is paying attention to us," I assured her.

She looked at me like a child who was just caught stealing candy, and it made me laugh out loud. She laughed too and her pussy tightened around me with every breath of her laugh. I took the opportunity to slam inside her hard and she gasped again, concern returning to her face.

"Will it help if I talk to you so people don't think my hard dick is inside you right now?" Her pussy gushed as I said the words of what we were doing out loud. Her face was still tense and so I slowed down my strokes.

"Baby, look around," I suggested.

She followed my instructions.

"See, no one has any clue," I said matter-of-factly.

"No one ..." I said as I pushed deep inside her then pulled halfway out.

"Has any ..." Another deep pump inside. She gasped.

"Clue!" I said louder, pushing myself deep inside her once more.

She moaned in pleasure as her eyes rolled back into her head. I kissed her softly and kept my mouth on hers as I picked up my pace. She relaxed in my arms as I moved in and out of her under the water. After a few minutes she matched her hip rhythm to mine.

"Hold on, baby, stop," she said. "I want to do it." I smiled.

I grabbed onto the side of the pool. Her arms wrapped around my neck and she slowly tilted her hips, taking me deeper and deeper inside of her as she got the hang of fucking underwater. It was quite the sensation to get used to, as the water worked against us, but that only made her grip feel tighter around my dick. Her pussy pulsated and I knew she was getting close to climax. I wanted to cum together for our first time, and with her pussy talking to me again, it wasn't hard to get on her level.

"Baby, I want us to cum together. When you're about to cum, put your mouth against mine and as you're cumming, give me your moans so that no one hears. I'm ready when you are."

And with my words, as if I had spoken directly to her pussy, her walls pulled on my dick as I went in and out. I pulled my dick all the way out so that just the tip was inside her and then in one firm, upward movement, slammed my hard dick all the way, deep into her pussy. She put her mouth on mine and the grip of her pussy was enough to pull my orgasm out of me as she moaned from deep within her into my mouth. We came for the first time in unison, at this point not really caring if anyone was around to see.

For moments, we breathed as one as we both came, our open mouths pressed together. As soon as we were finished, I pulled out of her and pulled her close to me, kissing her hard and driving my tongue deep into her mouth. There in that pool, we made our love official, sealed with a kiss.

Lena

"I love you, too," I said to Jay after pulling out of our kiss. He smiled a huge smile at me.

"I was just starting to wonder how many more times I could make you lose your breath before you were able to finally say it back," he joked. "Those words coming from your lips have never sounded sweeter."

"Come on, I'm not finished with you yet," he said, and my pussy did another somersault. I grabbed my completely saturated towel and wrapped it tighter around me as Jay pulled me toward the shallow end until my feet could reach the bottom of the pool. We emerged seemingly undetected and headed for our room. Once inside, Jay yanked my towel off me playfully, exposing, once again, my naked body.

"I'm not sure if I'll ever quite get used to this view," he said as he stood there admiring me, his own towel on the floor near his ankles. His hard dick stuck straight out in front of him. His body, so muscular and chiseled, was so sexy. And so mine. My pussy got wet again at the thought.

Jay walked toward me slowly. He walked around behind me, not taking his eyes off me and hugged me from the back. All I could feel was his dick pressing against the top of my ass. He wrapped his arms around my stomach and sucked on the top of my shoulders. I reached behind me and grabbed his dick with both hands, feeling his thickness in my hands for the first time. My pussy throbbed at the thought of this dick being all mine.

Suddenly Jay put his hands on my shoulder blades and pushed, bending me over while my hands just barely made it to catch myself from landing face first on the bed. There was that aggression again that turned me the fuck on. With the bed underneath me, I leaned on my forearms for support, my feet on the floor.

"Grab your right ankle with your right hand," he directed me, "and hold yourself up with your left."

I did as I was told and braced myself for whatever he was going to do next. This man always kept me guessing. I felt his whole hand slide between my pussy lips and up to rub my clit. There was something so sexy in the way his big hand grabbed my small, little pussy, all his for the taking.

I bent my chin toward my chest and peered between my legs to watch his fingers going to town on my clit. He then removed his hand, gathering wetness with him as he went, and rubbed it all over the head of his dick, already dressed with a condom. He grabbed the base, positioned the head on my pussy and slammed deep inside my juicy center as I screamed out in pleasure.

His dick felt twice as big in doggy style and I could feel him in my stomach. It took a minute to get used to the angle with my hand around my ankle as I began to push my ass back at him. His hands grabbed my ass and spread my cheeks open as he pounded away at my pussy. Relentlessly, he pounded, as I squeezed my muscles around him with each stroke.

He slowed down as he slid his dick nearly all the way out of me and then WHAM! he slammed all the way inside me, causing my pussy to squirt. He stopped for a second, taking in what had just happened and realizing that not only was this pussy extra juicy, but it squirted too. My pussy smiled a self-satisfied smirk.

I had pushed him out of me when I squirted, so he slid his dick back inside as he bent over me and grabbed my tits in his hands. I let go of my ankle to position my arms underneath me for support as I once again rested on my forearms. Jay moved my leg so my knee was propped on the edge of the bed.

He gave a few pumps and then squeezed my nipples as he pulled almost all the way out of me and slammed his dick hard into my pussy, making me squirt again. The bed beneath me was soaked as he continued to make me squirt over and over. Eventually, things got so wet that each time he slammed his dick inside me, my juices splashed, soaking both of us in my liquids. I could barely catch my breath as each time I prepared to squirt I held my breath, allowing myself to focus on squeezing all of my muscles around him.

He continued to pump and pump, eventually splashing my cum in my own face as I watched myself between my legs, squirting over and over. Never had my own juices got in my own eye before and I couldn't help but to giggle. I knew he was about to cum when he kept steady, no longer focused on making me squirt.

Rhythmically, I bounced my hips up and down as he began to breathe heavily before he screamed out, "Lena, I'm about to cum, baby! Don't stop!"

Moments later he collapsed on top of me and we lay on the bed, soaking wet. I couldn't move as I tried to stop myself from shaking with the aftershocks that my body made involuntarily. We lay there until the wet bed got cold.

Jay

For the rest of the weekend, we could not stop fucking like animals. We ordered room service and stayed in, enjoying each other's naked company and taking care of each other's every need. When it was time for Lena to fly back to the city, I gave her a mission, should she choose to accept. I challenged her to, in the next few days, sleep with Luke one last time to make sure she truly was ready to give up the single life and all the immature little boys in it. I wanted her to believe once and for all that after a weekend like the one we had just shared, in no way was she was the reason for Luke's sad lack of performance. I knew it would be a slam dunk.

Lena

After one of the best weekends I've ever had, I flew back home, knowing that I had just committed to the ride of my life. I could not wait to tell Matt at work all about my wild weekend with Jay, now officially my boyfriend.

When I got to work on Monday morning, as luck would have it, the first person I ran into when I got off the elevator was Luke. He asked me how my weekend was and all I could do was respond with a deep sigh.

"It was the best," was all I could muster.

He looked at me and cocked his head to the side as I sat at my desk. He kept walking, and as soon as he was out of earshot, I stood and draped myself over the divider between Matt's desk and mine.

"You let him hit it," was the first thing out of Matt's mouth as he smiled up at me.

"Don't say it like that, jerk!" I teased with a snarky tone. "Actually, he admitted that he was in love with me and THEN, yes, we made love."

"Ooooh, go Lena!" he teased back. "Well, shit. Finally!"

"Oh my God, it was SO worth the wait, Matt, you have no idea. I'm in love!" I said in a dramatic tone with an equally dramatic full body collapse into my chair.

He chuckled. "You're an idiot."

He stood, likely wanting to see if he could make fun of me for falling out of my chair. "Well hey, I'm happy for you. Now can I finally meet this dude? I'm a bigger fan of his than you are." He winked.

"Yeah, yeah, in due time, buddy. For now, he's all mine!"

Matt rolled his eyes as he sat back down.

Before the next weekend, I accepted Jay's challenge and fucked Luke one last time. Correction: I tried to fuck him one last time. He failed miserably at keeping his dick hard, again, nervous as always, palms sweaty, heart beating almost audibly. I couldn't even stand to be next to him any longer, and I never looked back afterward.

When I told Jay I had taken on his challenge, he asked me one simple question:

"So it's official then ... you're all mine?"

I nodded my head with a smile. "I am allllllllll yours, Jay!"

Oh King Solomon

Draya

We met Solomon out one night at the largest club in Atlantic City. This particular club had three separate floors, all with different vibes: the first floor had the largest bar in the place, where most people hung out and chatted; the second floor, a giant Top-40s dance floor with scantily clad dancers suspended in cages hanging from the ceiling; and the top floor, a room that reminded me of the "study" in the game *Clue*, with books and a fireplace and an old-school R&B vibe. The walls were mahogany and the chairs that framed the dance floor were leather. I immediately knew this room would be our spot.

As I scanned the crowd, I considered the mission my man had presented to me for the night. Oftentimes when we went out, I liked for him to give me missions to heighten our experience and give a purpose to the night so we could get the most out of our time together.

I saw Solomon standing by himself, seemingly alone. I first noticed his height and his muscular build, which was obvious through his white, button-down shirt and tight, dark denim jeans. My man aside, Solomon was definitely the yummiest man in the room and the excitement built inside me at once. I needed to have him on this dance floor.

Lincoln

That night in Atlantic City, my girl asked me for a mission before we got to the club. While I let her and her girl, Jada, get ready in their hotel room, I brainstormed in the adjacent man cave I got for myself. My challenge would be simple, but meaningful.

My girl and I hadn't been dating more than a few months, but I noticed she liked to play coy when we were out. This reserved side of her showed when we first began dating but I thought she was just nervous.

I asked her about this on occasion and she said although she could be shy at times, she purposely played the sexy coy role because she enjoyed when a man pursued her; it was easier. Of course it was easier to be pursued—that made her the rejecter, not the rejected. Thinking about the numerous talks we'd had on this topic, fear of rejection kept her from going after what she wanted, and I wished for her to have freedom from that fear. In anticipation of the night ahead of us, the mission became clear: my girl had to step out and become the aggressor.

Draya

While Jada and I were taking our time letting everyone get a glimpse of us and simultaneously stalking our prey, my man walked up behind us and handed us two vodka sodas. He then walked away, leaving us to our own devices. As Jada struck up a conversation with a cute, curly-haired, light-skinned girl nearby, I caught eyes with Mr. Tight Jeans.

I nervously flashed him a quick smile and he returned it with the most brilliant, toothy smile I had ever seen. His teeth were perfectly straight and strikingly white and immediately made my panties wet. Shy as all hell, I quickly turned away from him, unknowingly right in the direction of my man, who was watching the whole interaction from across the room.

Seeing the pathetic exchange, he closed his eyes and shook his head at me, followed by this look like, "Really, bitch, did you not understand the mission I gave you?"

Embarrassed, I shook it off and decided to see what Jada and her new friend were up to.

Lincoln

As we entered the room on the top floor, I headed right for the bar to grab us all drinks. Our routine is that no matter the mission, my girl spends the first few minutes familiarizing herself with her surroundings while I get the first round. I handed the girls their drinks and headed to a spot across the room where I could watch all the action.

My girl loved the mission I gave her and even convinced Jada to participate as well at being the aggressor for her own catch.

I got to my post and scouted potential dudes I thought my girl might choose. Her "type" was all over the place; she liked them tall and dark, but the rest seemed to depend on her mood and her vibe. I saw the perfect specimen not far away from the girls, giving my girl a look that could chew right through her.

It wasn't long before my girl's eyes landed on him, too, and I saw her give him her signature sexy, coy smile. He returned her gesture with a dazzling smile that almost made *me* wanna fuck him!

What she did next shocked the hell out of me—she turned away! I was in disbelief, yet thrilled she turned in my direction so I could chew her ass out with a simple look and disappointed head shake. She was clearly interested, otherwise she wouldn't have been so shy, and yet she missed the perfect opportunity to begin her mission.

Game on.

Draya

After prying Jada away from her new friend, Char, we headed to the bathroom to freshen up. I already needed to take a minute to gather myself. My heart pounded; it was only a matter of time before I had to put aside my foolishness and take action. No way was I going to endure the everlasting teasing from my man that would surely take place if I didn't go through with his mission, and I was no quitter!

Before I made my attack, I wanted to make sure my makeup was on point, my tits sitting up high, and hell, I even did a few squats in the handicap stall so my ass was extra perky and plump.

As we headed back to Char and her friends, I looked toward where Mr. Tight Jeans was standing to see none other than my man standing next to him, the two of them laughing! I shook my head in awe at his gall as I mumbled, "Shit!" under my breath. He must have guessed our previous exchange made my pussy throb, and of course had to take matters into his own hands.

As my mind swirled, I caught my man's gaze, rolled my eyes at him and gave him a big, sarcastic smile without Mr. Tight Jeans noticing. I couldn't imagine what they were talking about, but there was a lot of nodding in agreement, hand slapping, and laughing. All I could think of was, "I'm done for!" I had absolutely no idea what they were up to.

Then, before I knew it, Mr. Tight Jeans was walking right toward me.

Lincoln

The ladies headed toward the restroom, making sure to walk slowly past Mr. Tall and Dark, hips switching and tits all up and out, giving him a view many would kill for. He made sure to take full advantage of the view and watched them as they walked all the way across to the other side of the room.

As I watched my girl walk past him without saying anything, I knew I was going to have to push her. I made my way to where this young man was standing and introduced myself. I did not let him know who I was with, but instead made small talk with him. We began talking about the club and the crowd and just shooting the shit, cracking jokes and people watching.

My girl and Jada came back into the room. I caught my girl's eye, and her whole face changed from carefree and tipsy to shocked and nervous. With her eyebrows raised, she looked across at me with those unique hazel eyes of hers as if to say, "Man, baby, what are you up to?"

I was pushing her to take action by showing her how it's done, challenging her to take the reins, which were set up and now placed right in her hands.

I turned back to Mr. Tall and Dark and pointed in my girl and Jada's direction. "So what do you think of those two over there? We're all here as friends celebrating a birthday." He responded with that signature smile of his and asked a few questions about the tall one with the long, red hair and long legs with the ass popping in those skin-tight black pants.

My answer was simple, "She's very single, man, go get her!"

Permission granted, he turned and walked straight toward my girl.

Draya

At this point it was safe to say my heart was in my throat. With the image of my man's disappointed face burning behind my eyes, I did something I never would have expected of myself. Before Mr. Tight Jeans could say a word, I turned to face him straight on, and as he reached me I pushed my index finger against his lips. I set down my drink with my other hand and grabbed the back of his neck, pulling his face toward mine, and stuck my tongue all the way down his throat.

He moaned in what sounded like equal parts surprise and pleasure, slid his hands around my waist and pulled my body into his. I opened my eyes to see if I could catch my man's eyes, and his look of complete and utter shock made me giggle against Mr. Tight Jeans' mouth. He pulled away and flashed me an even bigger and more brilliant smile than he had before. My heartbeat pounded against my chest and I flashed him a huge smile in return.

"What's so funny, miss?" he asked.

Oh shit! I had no idea how I was going to get myself out of this one.

I blurted, "I was just picturing how differently that could have gone!"

"You mean if I didn't want you as badly as you want me?"

The question shocked the shit out of me and my pussy instantly tightened. The nerve of this man! Who is so arrogant to say that to someone whose name they don't even know?

Yet it was true, I wanted this man ... and bad.

"Solomon," he breathed into my ear, knocking me out of my thoughts.

I paused, taking in his fresh, musky scent, allowing a moment to collect myself.

"Draya," I whispered back.

"Well, Draya, it appears you need another drink." His hands still around my waist, he spun me around and walked behind me, his chest against me, pushing me to the bar. As soon as we got close, he spun me around again to face him and planted a huge kiss right on my mouth, sparing the tongue this time.

"So, what are you drinking?"

"Ketel soda, please," I responded, breathless.

He ordered one for each of us and we toasted to a great night.

Boy, would that prove to be an understatement.

The conversation flowed and the laughs weren't far behind. I was enjoying his company, but I wanted to check on

Jada and make sure she was good, so I politely excused myself. Despite the mission to be the aggressor, I was still a lady and did not want to come off as too easy or available, and wanted to mix up the energy so I wouldn't get bored.

Jada and Char were arm in arm, spilling drinks all over each other in between their uncontrollable laughter. She was obviously good, so I decided to have some fun.

I went out to the dance floor, where only a few people were getting their groove on. With lots of space all to myself, I swayed my hips to the beat of the Earth, Wind & Fire song that played through the speakers. With my drink in my hand, my whole world disappeared as I lost myself in the music. My man and Solomon watched me from opposite sides of the room, so I really got down and dirty.

If I knew my man at all, I could guess the hands that soon caressed my booty weren't his, as he would not want to sabotage the mission by scaring anyone off, especially after my kiss attack on a complete stranger.

I kept my eyes closed, enjoying the mystery of whose hands were now groping on the front of my thighs as a bulging dick pressed against my ass. I recognized the cologne I smelled as Solomon's. As we found our rhythm to a slow grind, I opened my eyes and saw my man beaming at us as he watched his girl being touched all over in front of him. It gave me a rush to know he was watching me back my ass up on another man. I leaned back into Solomon, exposing my neck to him so he could kiss and suck all over it.

My man kept the drinks flowing as he stood back and watched me work. He nodded encouragingly to me. I gave him a wink, stepped slightly forward and turned around to face Solomon, who glistened from sweat. I stepped forward into his ready arms with my arms around his neck and stuck my tongue down his throat once more. Our tongues danced aggressively around each other and the swelling in my pussy increased.

I pulled away and purred in his ear, "Follow my lead tonight and do what I tell you. Only stop if I tell you to, okay?"

He looked me dead in the face. "You got it, Draya."

His compliance turned me on so much I spun around once more to slam my ass back at him as the song switched and picked up the pace.

Facing my man, I lifted my drink in the air to toast him for challenging me with his mission and allowing me to grow into myself in this expressive way. I mouthed "thank you" and blew him a kiss. He grinned from ear to ear and winked back, not to be obvious that we were very much a couple. While I had his attention, I decided to surprise him.

I downed my own drink in a few gulps then grabbed Solomon's drink. For both of them to watch, I slowly poured his drink down the front of my chest. The cool liquid down my steaming body felt so good and gave me a chill that made my nipples harden. I grabbed one of Solomon's hands and with my hand on top of his, traced from my thigh, up the side of my torso underneath my loose-fitting cropped shirt, and firmly grabbed my right breast so he could feel the effect of his cold drink. He tugged on my hard nipples and his dick grew bigger against my ass. I enjoyed his large hand cupping and massaging my tits as he moved from one to the other.

Lincoln

My girl took my lead and introduced herself to Mr. Tall and Dark by tonguing him down. I had seen my girl kiss other dudes before, but this kiss was one I had not expected. I was so proud she finally had stepped up to the plate and gone after what she wanted.

As I watched my girl make her move, she shocked me even further when she opened her eyes mid-kiss and winked at me! My look of utter disbelief was enough to send her over the edge and she burst out laughing, ending her kiss attack on Mr. Tall and Dark. I then watched her playfully dodge the bullet that undoubtedly came in the form of a need to explain herself, which proved successful before she was whisked away toward the bar.

As I worked on the drink in my hand, I was able to relax for the first time all evening, knowing the mission was fully underway. I took in all around me, noticing for the first time how many couples were in the room with us. This made me feel at ease, knowing my girl and her new toy would fit right in and she would be comfortable testing her abilities to the fullest.

Out of the corner of my eye, a new entity entered the dance floor, but I was focused on other things and didn't pay the person much mind. As if trying to get my attention, the person danced right in my line of vision. It was my girl, alone, swinging her hips and touching all over herself in the middle of the room. I smiled hard, knowing she was feeling herself in the way I so loved to watch.

She was so beautiful, eyes closed, in her own little world. It was as if no one else was in the room, yet she was the focus of most. I just stared at her, the way her tight black pants hugged every curve, the gold zipper up the front swinging ever so slightly, her perky breasts directing her loose-fitting top back and forth to the beat. Confidence was pouring out of her and I couldn't take my eyes off of her.

While her eyes were still closed, Mr. Tall and Dark approached her from behind, groping on her ass before pressing himself against her backside. She slowly opened her eyes and smiled at me from across the room. She looked truly free, and I knew this would be a night neither of us would ever forget.

Watching my girl and Solomon getting it in on the dance floor got me excited. My love for this woman was so deep that her happiness truly brought me more joy than I could explain. Seeing her confidence strengthen as this man chased her around the club and the joy on her face every time we made eye contact made my heart swell for her. The kissing and groping and grinding only heightened my excitement and added an element of sexiness to the night.

As I watched my usually shy girl commanding this grown-ass man, my dick got harder and harder. I watched as she finished her drink, yet something in me told me to keep watching and ignore my natural instinct to head to the bar to get her a refill. She reached for his drink, which he handed over eagerly, and instead of bringing it to her lips, she slowly poured the entire thing down the front of her chest, soaking her shirt so it clung against her body, revealing how hard her nipples were from the ice. She grabbed his hand, and together they moved it up her thigh, along her torso, and underneath her shirt until she abandoned his hand to leave him to massage her perky tits.

She leaned herself back into him to rest her head on his shoulder, exposing her neck, and thrust her hips out so he could work his hand back down over her stomach. I simply couldn't pull my eyes off her and wanted to see what she would do with both hands free before I got her another drink. She reached down to the zipper that ran up the front of her leggings and slowly pulled it all the way down to where it stopped at the top of her pussy. His hands followed hers and she took his arm by the wrist, pushing his hand down the front of her pants so he could play with her clit in front of the entire club. Her eyes rolled to the back of her head and her entire body looked as if a ten-ton weight had been lifted off her.

Draya

I was so hot and bothered and my pussy so wet I had to feel Solomon's big hands inside me. As he rubbed all over my tits, I leaned back so he could get the best view, and angled my hips forward, taking down the zipper of my pants. His height towering over me allowed him to see all I was up to and his hands were soon moving south. I directed his hand down the front of my pants and nearly lost it as the tip of his fingers reached my clit. I closed my eyes as my pussy got wetter and wetter, throbbing harder and harder. Solomon's long finger entered me and the sensation immediately threw me over the edge. I gushed all over his hand. He moaned in my ear and I moaned out loud as his finger worked in and out of my pussy while I came. I would have lost my balance had it not been for Solomon's arms wrapped around my body holding me tightly against his.

As soon as I came out of the cloud, I opened my eyes. My man had been watching the whole thing. He nodded and smiled in encouragement and held his own drink up as a toast to me this time. The more I watched my man watching me being fingered, the more turned on I got as I gyrated and pushed back against Solomon along to the music.

Solomon in return reached both hands down my pants. He slipped a second finger inside me, shoving both deep inside my hot pussy, working his fingers in and out to the beat as his other hand spread my fat pussy lips apart so he could get better access to my clit. I had to grab both of his arms so I wouldn't fall face first onto the floor as his hands worked on my pussy like I had never felt before. The sensation of getting finger-fucked in public, my clit being rubbed sternly, and locking eyes with my man sent me into ecstasy once again. It took everything in my power not to close my eyes so I could stay connected with my man as my pussy leaked all over me from another man's hands.

As I watched my man get more and more excited by the show, I knew I had to turn things up.

I came so hard, and when I was done, I turned around to face Solomon, trying to act sexy, but really just to prevent myself from collapsing on the floor.

Facing each other, Solomon and I swayed together to the beat as I unbuckled his belt and undid his tight, dark, denim jeans. I felt on his stomach with one finger and traced the sexy V-cut that led right down to his package. The tips of my fingers found their way underneath the band of his boxer briefs and I lightly scratched at him, letting him know how badly I wanted to feel his hard dick in my hand. I reached further down his briefs and scratched at his pubic hair, knowing I was dangerously close to my goal. My hand lingered there for a few moments before I grabbed his thick shaft. It was so thick that when my fingers wrapped around it my fingertips were nowhere near touching.

He took small steps forward, pushing me backward toward the wall so I could really get to work. We were still the only ones on the dance floor, as the room had not yet begun to fill up, and I blindly trusted that he wouldn't allow me to bump into anyone had there been someone in our path. As soon as I felt the cold wall against my back, I shoved my hand all the way down his pants to feel his length. It felt even bigger and harder in my hand than it had against my ass and I couldn't help but to smile. I stroked his dick to the music as he took my face in his hands, brought it up to meet his and stuck his entire tongue into my mouth, initiating a passionate kiss.

I lightly bit his tongue as he pulled it out of my mouth and he let out a soft moan. I then took his massive dick out of his pants and placed it right on top of my pussy lips outside of my pants to let him know that if not for being in this club, I would have let him stick it all the way deep inside my hot, wet pussy with no hesitation.

Lincoln

To see my girl lose herself at the mercy of another man was the hottest thing I had ever seen. She exploded the moment he reached down the front of her pants. To see her familiar facial expressions from afar got my dick so hard. I wanted more ... much more.

She opened her eyes and looked directly at me, her hazel eyes piercing mine with a hunger I had never seen before. I lifted my glass to her and smiled, letting her know I was definitely enjoying the show and pushing her to take it further. She pushed herself back on Solomon and he in turn reached both hands down her pants, going to work inside her.

This time when she came, she did not break eye contact with me, as difficult as that looked for her with her entire body shaking from round two. As soon as she finished, she turned to face him.

It was time to break my trance. I headed for the bar, seeking out the sexy brunette bartender, Maisie. I ordered three Ketel sodas, one for myself, and the other two I requested that she take to my girl and Solomon. I did not want my presence to ruin the moment, and I knew my girl would appreciate the sexy eye candy.

As I made my way back to my front-row seat, Solomon had my girl backed up against the wall, the two of them staring at each other with my girl's hands down the front of his jeans, stroking his dick. He grabbed her face and tongued her down, pulling her whole body against his. She had found herself at this man's mercy, yet was completely in control with his manhood in her hands. Even though she had her back against the wall, he was entirely at her beck and call, and she was in her power. It was such a beautiful sight to see, my girl going after exactly what she wanted.

It mattered little to me that in the moment, what my girl wanted was the energy of another man; this experience was going to benefit her as a woman and us as a couple so much. She had always told me how she dreamt of having a big life, and with more experience than her, I knew the first step for her to get to that point was that she needed to become friends with the unknown and stop fearing rejection. She needed to take action and let her words follow, not the other way around. Solomon had no idea how lucky he was to be the focus of her desires for the night, yet he definitely took full advantage!

Draya

I felt a tap on my shoulder and saw the beautiful bartender who had greeted us at the beginning of the night. Maisie was like an angel from heaven, an oasis in the middle of the desert, with two drinks in her hand and a sexy, I-know-what-you're-up-to smile playfully dancing on her lips. Solomon and I separated our bodies slightly to be polite, but each kept a hand down each other's pants. Solomon directed her to put the drinks on the nearest table and thanked her, flashing her that dazzling smile that made everyone in its path swoon.

She responded with a sigh and a thank you, then glanced at me, raising her eyebrows and smiling in approval and envy. I smiled back shyly as she turned and walked away. I glanced back at Solomon and we both burst out laughing at being caught. We looked around for the culprit of the gracious drinks and both noticed my man at the same time. He smiled and saluted us as Solomon mouthed, "Thanks, man!" I puckered my lips and kissed the air at him. Boy, I loved that man so much.

Solomon moved his fingers inside me and watched as I was pulled back into the moment. He smiled so big.

"Hi, Draya," he said to me, in the same tone he used when we first introduced ourselves after my kiss slaughter.

"Hi, Solomon," I mouthed back with a smile.

What he said next made my pussy tighten around his fingers.

"I want you to cum with me, Draya."

I nearly lost it. I stroked his dick firmly and steadily as his hands worked all over my pussy. As my pussy walls throbbed, alerting him I was about to climax, he quickened his pace, driving me over the edge as his dick pulsated in my hands. Our releases were simultaneous, the music drowning out our moans. My cum dripped down my leg, but I caught his cum with my hand so he wouldn't mess up his shirt.

We collapsed into each other, breathing heavily, letting both our heartbeats slow down to a normal pace. Solomon was the first to break away, as I was plastered against the wall, unable to move. He leaned down and kissed me gently, then bent down to retrieve our drinks that didn't stand a chance against all we had just experienced. He handed me the napkins that Maisie had placed under each glass to wipe my hands with. I had gotten out of Solomon exactly what I wanted.

Solomon and I reluctantly pulled ourselves out of our own little pleasure corner and joined up with Lincoln, Jada, and Char. As a reward for stepping out of my comfort zone and commanding what I wanted that night, my man encouraged me to remain with Solomon for the rest of the night. He wanted me to relish my own success so that I could feel the confidence that came along with going after and attaining what I desired. I was on a high for the entire evening. Mission accomplished.

The next morning, as we lay in bed enjoying each other's lazy company, Lincoln turned on the TV. It was preset to the news, and while we waited for our room service, I noticed the headline on the bottom of the screen: *King of Africa to hold conference in AC Casino.*

"Baby, look!" I sat up straight, gathering the blankets to cover my naked body.

Lincoln rolled over and lifted his head to see the screen. A video of Solomon surrounded by men in dark suits walking into a casino played across the TV.

"Holy shit," he responded with genuine admiration. I looked down at him to see him smiling up at me, the tone in his voice directed toward me. "You made an African king cum all over himself, baby, I'm impressed," he teased.

"I'm speechless," was all I could muster, a dumb grin coloring my face.

"No words needed. I want you to think about his big dick while I make you cum now. Don't take your eyes off that screen so long as he's on it."

I lay back as Lincoln's head disappeared underneath the sheets.

Famous Last Words

Mike

"Baby, would you ever be interested in having a threesome?" my girlfriend, Naya, blurted out in the car on our way to dinner.

We were headed to Las Vegas the next morning for business presentations I had to give and didn't want to be bothered with dishes and cleaning before we left.

"Well that was out of left field," I responded once my laughter subsided.

Naya and I had been together for over a year and it never ceased to surprise me when a new fantasy arose. I had learned early on in our relationship that Naya was far more receptive to talking about desires and fantasies when I gave her the space and time to bring them up on her own. But I'd learned once she put something on the table, even if it was just an innocent question, she wanted me to help her make whatever it was come to life.

"What made you think of that?" I asked. Her questions were always inspired by something she saw, or a conversation she was a part of.

"I don't know ..." She shrugged. "I came across an Instagram page of this girl who is in a relationship with both a guy and another girl. It seems so normal to them, the two girls sharing a man ... It just got me thinking about what it would be like."

We pulled up to the restaurant and valeted the car. As always, I requested a booth so we could sit next to each other. As soon as we placed our order with the waitress, the conversation from the car intensified. Naya had never had a threesome before, and knowing I had, she peppered me with all types of questions.

"Do you prefer two girls or a girl and another guy?"

"They're completely different experiences."

"How so?"

"Well ... with two girls in the same room, it's a bit of a juggling act for the dude because girls tend to get jealous," I explained. "The guy has to make sure both chicks feel like they're getting enough attention. With two dudes, it's a lot less psychological."

"But which one do you prefer?" she asked, digging deeper for details.

"It depends on the people, baby. If the two girls are into each other, then I prefer two chicks. The woman, or women, involved have to be happy and satisfied. That's really the only way I've found any kind of threesome to work. Once you females get in your feelings, the whole thing goes to shit." I rolled my eyes and shook my head. "Could you see yourself being with a woman?"

"Kind of ... Growing up and even throughout college I always said, 'I'd let a girl go down on me, but I could never

ever eat a girl out.'" She played with her napkin and brushed her hair behind one ear. "But now I think if it was with the right girl I might be able to. It'd have to be with someone I really vibe with, though ..." she added, deep in thought.

"Well the good thing is that both girls don't need to go down on each other for it to be considered a threesome. You don't have to do anything you don't want to."

"Well, we'll see, maybe with enough liquor in me I'd be more open."

This was the first fantasy Naya had ever brought up that would not be something I could set up. It felt strange knowing that for the first time, I could not give her something she wanted. This experience would have to find her.

"Do you want to see me with another girl, baby?" she asked me, a seductive look in her eye. "Would it turn you on?"

"To see you enjoying yourself turns me on. If the right girl comes along that you want to explore with, then hell yeah, it would turn me on."

"And would it turn you on to see another girl eating my pussy, baby?" She fidgeted in her seat.

"Of course it would ..."

"And would it turn you on to see me tasting another girl's pussy?" she continued, her hands rubbing up and down her thighs as she moved closer to me so our bodies were touching.

I looked around to see if anyone was paying us any mind, and to my relief, no one was. "I'd love to see that pretty face of yours covered in another chick's cum, baby."

Naya pulled her skirt up and played with herself under the table. She leaned in close to me and in my ear whispered, "And would it turn you on to see me fuck another girl with my fingers?"

I looked over at her and saw her doing just that to her own pussy. I silently prayed our food would not come before my girl did. I leaned in and ran my tongue along the edge of her ear before sucking gently on her neck.

"Nothing would turn me on more than to see you make another girl cum, baby. She better make you cum first though, I want to see exactly what you look like when someone else makes your body go into convulsions as you cum all over the place."

With those words, she dug her face into my neck as she began breathing heavily, her body twitching slightly as she came at the dinner table.

Naya

The thought of having a girl-on-girl experience was enough to send me over the edge. I wasn't sure if it was because of how much I knew it would turn Mike on, or how much it might turn me on. Either way, as soon as he admitted how badly he wanted to see what I look like when someone else made me cum, I exploded all over myself under the table. Just as I caught my breath, the waitress came by with our food. As soon as she left, Mike leaned in close to me once again.

"I can't wait until the day you allow me to witness you fucking another chick. My dick is hard at the thought of it," he admitted.

I looked down at his lap and saw the massive dick print through his pants. A devilish grin danced across my lips as I looked up at him.

"I'll make sure not to find her without you, then," I

teased playfully, reaching over to rub on his dick. It was so hard underneath my hand, my pussy throbbed again. I thought about how badly I wished for Mike to push everything off this table and fuck me right here and now.

"You're so mine when we get home," I promised.

There's nothing like watching a man to whom you just promised pussy try to eat a meal at a normal pace.

We finished in record time. Mike slid a hundred dollar bill under the salt shaker, getting the attention of the waitress to let her know cash was on the table as we jetted out of there. No doubt she would be surprised when she saw at least a 100% tip waiting for her.

I could barely wait until we got to the car to unzip Mike's pants and take his dick out. Thankfully, we were only minutes from home. As soon as we got in the house and Mike closed the front door behind us, I dropped to my knees, taking his whole dick in my mouth. I grew wetter and wetter as I thought about lying on my back, another woman licking on my clit until I screamed out in pleasure while Mike watched.

All of a sudden, Mike lifted me off my knees and carried me to the nearest couch, laying me on my back as he pushed my skirt up around my waist and slid deep inside me. My breathing quickened as he pounded at my pussy relentlessly with his hard dick.

Just as I started to climax, Mike said, "Baby, I'm gonna cum!" He slammed his dick hard inside me one last time before he pulled out and came all over my pussy. He then quickly pulled his shirt over his head, wiped himself off, and slammed his still hard dick into me again, pushing me over the edge as I gushed all over him. He collapsed on top of me as we both caught our breath. After a couple minutes he got up and helped me to my feet.

"Come on, dirty girl," he said with a grin, "let's go take a shower."

The next morning, I packed our bags while Mike went to go pick up my friend Eva before we headed to the airport. Mike had a major presentation to give for one of his projects while in Vegas, so he suggested that I invite a friend to hang out with while he was busy working, and choosing Eva was a no-brainer. Although she and Mike had only met a couple of times, she would be the absolute perfect person to join us.

Eva and I had gone to high school together but were never really that close at the time. I was a late bloomer and was always intimidated by Eva's confidence and lust for life. She was part of the popular crowd and was always the life of the party. We lost touch when we both went to college, but soon after, a mutual friend reconnected us.

This time, something just clicked. I had matured greatly and now, years later, I could appreciate Eva in a way I was always too insecure to before. If anyone's personality belonged in Vegas with us, it was hers. She had been talking lately about how she needed an "escape weekend," having been dogged by the latest dude she was messing around with, and so she eagerly accepted our invitation.

As soon as we got to the hotel, Mike informed us he had booked Eva and I our own suite. Not only did he want space to work, but being the gentleman that he was, he also wanted to allow Eva the privacy from us as a couple if she so desired.

Eva and I were excited to be able to spend quality time together without having to worry about getting in Mike's way while he worked, and Mike was surely happy with his own space away from us girls. Our rooms were right down the hall from each other and we all went to put our bags away and get ready for dinner.

Mike

I got situated in my private room away from the ladies and immediately remembered a hotel tradition Naya and I kept. I called over to their room and Eva picked up the phone.

"Hey, Eva, can you put Naya on the phone for me?"

"She's in the shower, hold on ..." She called to Naya in the other room, followed by Naya's indistinct response.

"She told me to tell you to come here and she'll probably be out by the time you get here."

"It's okay. When she gets out of the shower, tell her I need to speak with her and I'll wait for her in my room."

Only minutes later, I heard a knock on my door. When I opened it, Naya stood there in thigh-high stiletto boots that made her stand at least six feet tall. Her hair hung down her back, still wet from her shower. The only other thing adorning her body was one of the white hotel towels.

"Leave it to my girl not to put any clothes on when summoned down the hall to my room," I thought to myself as I surveyed her from head to toe.

I took a few steps backward into the room and pulled the door open all the way, inviting her in without a word. She took a small step forward, just past the threshold of the door before letting her towel drop to the floor.

"You needed to talk to me about something?" she asked matter-of-factly.

Her body was completely hairless and glistening from the coconut oil she puts on after she showers. I was speechless as I stared her dead in the eye. She raised an eyebrow at me before kicking her towel to the side and pushing the door closed behind her.

She took long strides into the room with legs that went from the floor to the ceiling. She stopped in front of me and without saying a word, pulled my sweats down, exposing my hard dick that was tenting my sweatpants at the mere sight of her. It stuck straight out in front of me, reaching for her, and she grabbed it with both hands.

"Perhaps it would be better if you showed me?" she suggested, knowing I asked her here for one thing and one thing only.

I grabbed her by the wrist, spun her around and bent her face down on the bed, shoving my hard dick into her tight little pussy, wasting no time. I pounded away at my girl's pussy, slapping her hard on the ass, making her grow wetter and wetter. I grabbed a handful of her damp hair and pulled her head back gently, forcing her to arch her back as I slammed my dick deep inside her. I grabbed her hard by the hips and fucked her hard and fast, hitting her G-spot as her moans got louder. The deeper my dick got, the wetter her pussy got.

"Oh, fuck," she moaned through clenched teeth. "Right there, baby, make me cum," she begged.

I focused on her G-spot with the head of my dick and continuously hit it as her pussy throbbed and tightened around my dick. She reached her hand in between her legs and played with her clit. Not moments later she stopped making any noise, focusing as she prepared to cum.

"Cum on this dick, baby," I commanded her. "Give it

to me, baby, let it go," I urged.

She let out a deep moan and yelled out, "Oh my God, I'm cumming!" Her moans and screams could no doubt be heard all the way down the hall as her pussy gushed all over my dick and dripped down her inner thighs. I came right afterward, completely overwhelmed by the wetness surrounding my throbbing dick.

As soon as we were both finished cumming all over each other, I helped Naya to her feet, steadying her on her stilettos. She turned to face me and gave me a deep-throat tongue kiss as she grabbed the back of my neck.

"Great talk, baby," she said as she pulled away from me and walked away toward the door. She bent over and grabbed her towel off the ground, wrapped it around herself, and then opened the door. I followed behind her, wanting to watch her walk to her room. Halfway down the hall, she stopped and looked back at me over her shoulder.

Slowly, she ran both her hands down her torso and leg, folding her body forward, keeping her legs straight until she touched her toes, exposing her pussy lips to me from underneath the back of her towel. It was so juicy looking and raw, having just been beaten up.

My dick got hard again as I watched her get down on her hands and knees in the middle of the hall. I turned around to see if anyone else was in the hallway before I walked toward her.

She poked her ass up in the air and still looking back at me, spread her pussy lips open with her fingers for me to see. I dropped to my knees and shoved my dick back inside her and fucked her right in the hallway until she came again all over me. It took her less than a minute, as she always got off on the fear factor of being caught fucking in public.

Thankfully, no one came out of his or her room to catch us, but as I helped Naya back on to her feet, I noticed a camera staring straight at us. Hotel security surely got quite the show. I slapped her hard on the ass. She squealed and ran away toward her room.

Naya

We stayed at the Palms Casino, which had five different nightclubs. We figured because we were far removed from the strip, this first night we would take it easy and stay local. We grabbed dinner at one of the steakhouses and afterward decided to check out the rooftop bar. Knowing we were only an elevator ride away from our rooms, we hit the bar hard.

After the royal pounding Mike put on my ass earlier this afternoon, I was on fire. The sexual energy surrounding me was tangible, and it didn't take long for Eva to pick up on it. I grabbed her onto the dance floor and we got closer and closer as we danced. We finished our drinks and went to go find Mike by the bar. He was enjoying a cigar and admiring the Vegas skyline near a large, plush white couch.

After working up a bit of a sweat with Eva, the open air felt even better than it had when we first got to the roof. Each breeze sent a shiver down my spine and the cool air tickled my pussy lips, unconfined due to my lack of panties.

We grabbed another round of drinks and then Eva and I took a seat on the couch. I was mid-sentence when the look on Eva's face said she was no longer listening to what I was saying. Suddenly, she leaned in toward me and kissed me hard on the mouth, staying there without moving, judging my reaction. Eva and I had never been physical before and so I allowed it, wanting to feel how it felt to be kissed by her. It didn't take but a second for me to realize I liked it … a lot. I opened my lips slightly and her lips mimicked mine.

She stuck her tongue in my mouth before pulling away to look at me. She must have seen the hunger in my eyes as she drove her tongue back deep into my mouth. Our tongues swirled around each other desperately as if they had a thirst that could not be quenched. She put her hand on my thigh and leaned in closer to me as I grabbed the back of her neck and pulled her toward me.

Just then, Mike's weight lowered the couch next to me. I slid my hand from Eva's neck down her back and onto her ass. With my other hand, I grabbed her thigh and pulled her onto my lap so that she straddled me.

Our lips never broke for even a second as the passion between us intensified. I reached over and put my hand on Mike's thigh before pulling away from Eva and giving Mike a deep tongue kiss. When I pulled away, hunger lit Eva's face as she watched Mike and I tongue kiss in front of her.

I pulled away. "Stick your tongue down her throat, baby," I urged Mike. "I wanna see you kiss each other."

Mike leaned forward, grabbed a handful of Eva's long brown hair behind her head and pulled her face toward his, shoving his tongue deep into her mouth. She moaned audibly as she leaned her face further into his, pushing Mike's tongue back into his mouth and driving her tongue into it.

I ran both my hands up Eva's thighs on either side of mine, and dug both my thumbs into the creases at her hips, squeezing hard before moving my hands up Eva's torso and grabbing two large handfuls of tits as she continued to kiss my man.

My pussy got wetter and wetter the more I watched Eva and Mike kiss, inches away from my face. I reached over and grabbed Mike's thigh again, and waited for the opportunity to enter into a three-way kiss. With the liquor flowing heavily through my veins, I could not tell whose tongue was whose as we all shared a sloppy kiss together.

My pussy throbbed at this unexpected aggression between us and I didn't want to wait any longer to have my pussy touched. At this point, I didn't care whose hand would be the one to touch me. Suddenly, Eva reached between my legs. She scooted her ass back so she could have better access, and Mike pulled away from our kiss, leaving Eva and I to continue. He came over and sat on the other side of us to shield us from any onlookers, but it didn't take long before security came over and broke us up.

They must have recognized Mike and me from the security cameras, and our latest actions sealed our fate. They escorted the three of us toward a back room and proceeded to tell us we had to leave and were no longer allowed in the clubs or bars in the hotel.

They tried to ban us from the hotel itself, but Mike took the head of security to the side and had a word with him. Despite pulling out his corporate card and attempting to undo the damage, he could not undo all of it, but at least they allowed us to stay in our rooms and didn't get the police involved for indecent exposure.

Mike

The girls ran to the elevators hand in hand like children who just got away with stealing a cookie from the cookie jar as I calmly followed. I was slightly indignant; after all, this was Vegas, but I was too lit to make a further issue out of it with all we had already gotten away with. So long as the girls were safe, and none of my presentations were affected, I was good.

It was already close to 3 a.m., so we decided to head back to the girls' room where we had champagne. Another tradition of mine and Naya's was to order a bottle from room service as soon as we got settled in case we happened upon an occasion that warranted some bubbly. This was clearly an occasion that called for celebrating, as we were not in a Vegas jail cell.

As soon as the elevator doors closed behind us, Eva took two steps toward Naya and shoved her tongue back down her throat. Eva had claimed my girl for the night, and I had no choice but to share. Naya's hands were feeling all over Eva's tight little body with a desperation I had never seen before. My dick got hard at the thought of how foreign this all was to Naya, having only ever drunk-kissed her girlfriends at parties back in college.

The elevator opened on our floor. I gently moved behind Naya and put my hands on her hips, pulling her slightly toward me. She pulled Eva with her, paying me no mind.

"Guys, this is us," I said, interrupting their kiss.

Naya took a small step backward, slightly uneasy on her heels, leaning into me as Eva grabbed her hand and led her into the hallway. As soon as we got into the room, I crossed to the mini bar and opened the bottle of champagne. Eva and Naya wasted no time in undressing each other. Clothes went flying everywhere in urgent desire.

I realized this was a party for two, and it was best for

me to sit back and enjoy the show. I didn't want to interrupt or ruin the vibe these two vixens had going, so I grabbed a champagne glass and the bottle and headed toward the other end of the room, where floor-to-ceiling windows displayed the entire Vegas strip. I poured champagne in my glass, set the bottle down on the table between two large chairs, and turned to watch the action.

Eva was the first to get Naya down on the bed, more out of submission than force. She climbed on top of Naya, kissing her and getting right back into the position they had been in when security came and broke things up a half hour or so before. This time, Eva put her hands on Naya's shoulders and pushed her onto her back, kissing Naya as she straddled her. Eva reached her hand underneath her and began to finger Naya again, and Naya's breath quickened.

Just then, Eva hopped off Naya, turned around, and positioned her pussy directly over Naya's face. She lowered her body down and spread her legs open further, her clit touching Naya's lips as she leaned forward and began to lick all over Naya's pussy, 69-style.

Naya brought her hands onto either side of Eva's ass and lifted her face to stick her tongue deep into Eva's pussy. The blood rushed to my dick as I watched my girl do everything to Eva she had talked about at dinner last night that had made her cum all over herself. I reached down and grabbed my dick, moving it to the side underneath my pants so it could comfortably grow bigger.

I took a seat in one of the chairs and sipped my champagne as I focused on Naya's face deep in Eva's pussy. Every so often, she would let her head drop back onto the bed in pleasure, allowing me, for the first time, to see what she looked like while being pleasured by someone else. I had never before had the chance to see the way her body reacted, as I had always been the one causing it to react.

The feeling I had watching Naya and Eva pleasure each other was unexpected; although I had always been a voyeur, I was watching my girl fuck another girl in front of me without needing to get involved. This was a fantasy of Naya's, and to have the honor of seeing it play out in front of my eyes was more than enough for me.

Naya could not get enough of Eva's body. After a few minutes of eating the pussy hanging over her face, she pushed Eva off of her and climbed on top. Eva fought back but finally gave in when Naya pinned her against the bed with her hands above her head. Naya slid her hands down Eva's arms and right onto her tits, bringing them together and sucking on both of her nipples. She massaged Eva's plump tits as Eva kept her hands above her head and spread her legs wide open on either side of Naya in clear invitation.

Naya

After Eva rode my face while on top of me, I wanted to take control. I had enjoyed the taste of Eva's pussy in my mouth, but I wanted to explore her body without the distraction of her tongue on my clit. I pushed her onto the bed next to me and got on top of her, pinning her to the bed until she submitted.

I had always caught myself staring at her tits in high school, and now here they were, staring right back. I took them both in my hands and my pussy throbbed as I massaged them, kissed them, and sucked on them. They were the perfect size, a small C-cup, and firm as hell. They sat perky on her small frame, and while she lay on her back they laid across her chest like two perfect water balloons.

She opened her legs wide, urging me to taste her again, but she wasn't going to get my tongue that easily this time. I kissed her stomach and ran my tongue all along her torso. She arched her back in anticipation. She moaned as I sucked her inner thighs. I softly blew directly on her clit as I positioned myself between her legs. I lay down on my stomach, my face inches away from her soaking wet pussy, and grabbed the front of her thighs, pulling her closer to me.

She squealed in surprise as I slowly slid one finger inside her and found her G-spot. Her pussy tightened around my finger as I moved it in and out of her repeatedly, flicking her G-spot every time I entered her. I couldn't wait anymore to taste the effect of my handiwork.

Before putting my tongue directly on her clit, I looked over to see Mike sitting in the chair a few feet away from us, stroking his dick. I immediately thought of our conversation at dinner last night and how much he said it would turn him on to see me tasting another woman and having her cum all over my face.

My pussy throbbed at the thought. I smiled at him suggestively before turning back to Eva and licking her from her tight little hole all the way up to her clit, gathering all of her juices in my mouth. I then spat it all on her clit before going to town on her with my tongue. Her clit swelled by the second as the blood rushed to her pussy. She lifted her hips to meet my face and fucked my mouth as I stuck out my tongue.

Mike

The urgency these two had to please each other fueled their aggression and could only be described as fuck fighting. There was no romance in what Naya and Eva were doing to each other, but instead, a wrestling match of control and power over one another.

Neither of them let themselves reach climax, but instead reached the brink before going on the attack again. They took turns throwing each other on the bed, pinning each other down, breaking free from each other, neither of them knowing whether they wanted pussy in their mouth or a mouth on their pussy more.

I couldn't help but to unbutton my pants and stroke my dick as I watched Eva face fuck my girl on the bed right in front of me. Eva's arched back gave her body the shape of an S as her tits pointed straight up to the sky, her legs wrapped around either side of Naya's head.

Eva moaned with desire then slid her body up and away from Naya. Naya instinctively grabbed Eva's ankles, pulling her body back down and her pussy back into Naya's mouth. Eva moaned deeply, distracted by Naya's tongue, and allowed her to suck on her pussy for a few more seconds.

Then, she forcefully broke free from Naya's grip. As Naya crawled up toward Eva, Eva pushed Naya's chest down onto the bed, her ass sticking straight up into the air. Eva quickly crawled behind Naya and ate her pussy from the back, running her tongue up and down from Naya's clit to her ass. Naya spread her legs wide open, allowing Eva to shove her tongue deep inside her.

At this point, I was the first one to cum, as I busted my

nut all over the floor in front of me. The second Naya heard my deep moans, she moaned as well, no longer able to hold herself back as she came all over Eva's face.

As soon as Naya had finished cumming, she immediately made it her mission to make Eva cum. She flipped over and lay on her back, pulling Eva on top of her so Eva was sitting directly on her face. Naya grabbed two handfuls on Eva's ass and spread her cheeks open, creating space for her to shove her whole face in Eva's pussy. Eva let out a deep sigh as she reached for the wall in front of her to steady herself on top of Naya.

Naya massaged Eva's ass while she repeatedly pulled her hips forward. Eva slid her pussy back and forth over Naya's face. Naya spit and slurped Eva's pussy juices, audibly revealing how wet she was. My dick was still hard and I could feel myself about to cum again. Naya moaned, the vibrations resonating on Eva's pussy. She rocked back and forth against Naya's face until she gushed all in Naya's mouth. From the sounds she made, Eva and I came in unison.

I never thought I could feel so connected to two people I wasn't touching.

Eva collapsed on the bed next to Naya as they both caught their breath. I pulled my briefs up over my waning erection and walked over to the mini bar, grabbed two more flutes, and poured them each a glass of champagne. They lay in bed together as I undressed and got into the other bed. We laughed and talked for a while before Eva dozed off to sleep. Naya put their empty champagne flutes on the nightstand before crawling into the other bed with me. She kissed me softly and I tasted Eva on her lips before she drifted off to sleep in my arms.

The next morning, I opened my eyes and saw that Eva was awake in the other bed, knees bent up under the covers and legs slightly apart. I figured she was on her phone. She saw me stir and looked over at me, propping herself up on her elbow.

"Thank you for sharing her with me last night," Eva whispered. "She is so delicious, I can't stop thinking about how sweet her pussy tastes." She lay back down on her back.

I spotted her phone on the nightstand. Eva was not on her phone at all, but was playing with herself under the blankets.

Morning wood turned serious.

"I wanna play with myself as I watch how a grown man fucks a woman the right way," Eva requested.

My dick grew harder at the thought of being inside Naya's pussy, surely still juicy from last night's fuck fest.

Naya was sleeping on her stomach. I sat up and slowly slid her legs apart. She moaned slightly but didn't wake up when I moved the sheets, exposing her ass. I slid my thumb between her legs to confirm she was still soaking wet. I positioned myself on top of her and gently slid my dick inside her. Half sleeping, Naya lifted her head from one side of the pillow to the other and another small moan escaped her mouth. I effortlessly moved in and out of her tight, wet pussy until she stirred. She began lifting her ass to meet me with every stroke.

I met Eva's eyes as she watched me fuck Naya awake. Eva's hand moved under her blanket and her breath quickened. She squirmed down the bed in order to get a better view.

Eva played with herself as she watched my dick disappearing over and over inside Naya's pussy. The harder Naya moaned, the more Eva moaned and the closer we all got to climax. Naya's pussy pulsated around my dick. I looked over at Eva to signal it was time. Naya was the first to start cumming as I quickened my pace, her moans causing a chain reaction as Eva came and then me, moments after.

"Take it easy," we said. "It's only our first night in Vegas." The three of us laughed for the rest of the weekend at how greatly we underestimated those famous last words.

We were all so fired up, having set the bar high for the weekend. I aced my presentations, and when I got back home, I received a promotion at work for how much I impressed the clients. Naya and Eva spent the weekend playing with each other at every chance they got. They were addicted to each other, and although I never touched Eva all weekend, it was the greatest threesome I had ever had.

P.A.S.S.I.O.N.

Sarah

> Felt passion... have you really?

The text appeared across my phone screen for the third time this week as I sat at my desk Wednesday morning. The texts came from the same 917 area code around the same time every day this week. I was utterly distracted by this habitual text. For the last two days I had tried to ignore it as a wrong number, but a third time was intentional. I decided to contact my girlfriends I had gone out with this past weekend to try to figure it out.

I switched from this random text to our group chat.

> Ok, I need your help. Either of you remember me giving my number out on Saturday night? I seem to have acquired an anonymous stalker. Lunch on me for anyone available to help play detective. Luxe Hotel Rooftop — 12:30pm xo

Brie was the first to arrive, and JC strolled in about ten minutes after I did. I ordered us a round of drinks in hopes alcohol would jog our memories from the hazy Saturday past. Neither Brie nor JC remembered me giving my number to anyone, not even the tall, funny guy who had been stuck at our table like white on rice. Brie, the most outgoing of us all, did not waste time in urging me to text the number back.

"Obviously if you've had to call an emergency meeting, Sarah, you're curious! Stop being such a scaredy-cat and figure out who this little secret admirer of yours is!"

"Secret admirer, yeah right!" I scoffed, the color coming into my cheeks. "More like a creep who won't leave me alone!" I joked.

"Maybe it was that group of dudes a few tables away who kept sending over drinks ..." JC suggested.

"But how would they get your number? They barely even said 'hi,'" Brie added. None of it really made any sense, but it was becoming increasingly obvious I would need to text the person back if we were going to get any real answers.

"Oh man, were we talking shit, though!" JC exclaimed with a huge smile. "Dudes can be so lame, and yet they keep on trying. We'd mention how pathetic they were right in front of them, and they would try even harder." She rolled her eyes dramatically.

I added with a chuckle, "Brie, you even laughed in that one guy's face, and he still wouldn't leave you alone all night! What a sad, sad, species men are!"

We all laughed at the memory of Saturday night. No matter how much I tried, though, I could not shake the feeling from these texts. At the mention of it, I had a strong feeling they were from the dudes at the other table pretending not to sweat us. The worst part of all was, none of us remembered what any of them looked like.

   With my curiosity overwhelming me and two nagging best friends in my ear, I decided to text this stranger back. I didn't want to give this person any further opportunity to play with me, so I got right to the point.

> Is this one of the guys sitting a few tables away from me and my girls on Saturday who was obviously too shy to come over and say hi?

> It might be, if you want it to be.

   This guy wanted to get on my nerves already. I read the response to the girls and then got busy typing.

> Well I want it to be.

> Good guess. Now which one of us is it? And tell me how I got your number...

   I read the response out loud to the girls, and we all looked at each other in bewilderment. None of us had any clue how this guy could have gotten my number without knowing us or asking for it, and we barely even remembered what these guys looked like, because we had other guys in our ears the whole night. This was starting to get weird, but we were all definitely intrigued. Did we really have that much to drink? As we pondered, the waitress showed up with the next round of cocktails.

"Did you order these?" JC asked me, her face scrunched up with confusion.

"Hell no, I'm already tipsy and have to get back to the office. Another drink and I might as well kiss that promotion goodbye!" We all burst out laughing.

Just then, my phone beeped with another text. I hadn't responded, but this guy was clearly not about to wait for my response.

> It's fine if you don't know. Maybe we can change that if you're interested.

Like a giddy schoolgirl, I read the girls the text and they both looked at me expectantly. At another *beep*, I looked down at my phone still in my hand.

> You might as well have given your number to the entire place when you told your girlfriends you'd been given a company phone with your promotion. Congratulations, by the way.

I blushed, embarrassed, and before I even looked up at Brie and JC, Brie grabbed my phone out of my hand and read the text out loud. They both looked from each other to me and burst out laughing. Had I really been that loud? Jesus, I was embarrassed, but at least this guy couldn't see me now! I played it cool.

> Damn, really? I gave my number out to the whole bar that night, huh? Well apparently my drunk ass has come back to haunt me because I seem to have found myself a stalker! But I like a little mystery, so if you play your cards right, maybe we can stay in touch. What's your name anyways so I can save it in my phone?

> I resent that comment, I'm no stalker. I just like what I like. But you haven't answered my question... have you ever felt passion?

There it was again, that repeated question. And then a second text.

> You made it clear that night that the men you deal with must have passion or some type of connection with you when you first meet. Do to really believe that bullshit?

I scoffed at the message and looked up at the girls with a shocked expression as I held my phone out for them to both read quietly.

"Damn, he's calling you out already, Sar!" Brie exclaimed.

I pulled my phone back and began typing.

> As a matter of fact, I do! And it's not bullshit. I can tell pretty quickly when a person is interested in me if I want to get to know them or not. Why are you asking, anyway?

I was trying to sound unbothered, but I had a feeling he could read right through it.

> My dudes and I were chuckling to ourselves that night because although what you were saying sounded good to those at your table, we could tell you ladies don't have a clue what you're talking about when it comes to passion or a connection with a real man.

> Oh, really now? What else did you overhear that you don't agree with, Mr. Know-It-All?

At this point, Brie was fidgeting in her seat, trying to get my attention. I hadn't realized how enthralled I had already become in the conversation.

"Ahem," she cleared her throat. "Although I'd love to see how this one ends, I have to get back to the office before Mr. Lawrence kills me. I've had one too many boozy lunch breaks this month, and he gets handsy when he knows I've been drinking. Life of a personal assistant." She rolled her eyes as she stood.

"Definitely wanna know more about this secret admirer of yours, girl. Text me later!" She blew a kiss to each of us and strutted her tight little body across the deck toward the elevators.

JC and I exchanged sly smiles, eager to get back to Mr. Know-It-All. We were too curious to waste any more time. I picked up my phone and saw a new message.

> If you want to hear all of what I have to say, I'll need your undivided attention. I'm finished with work today but don't want to assume you're free as well. Otherwise, we can do this another time. I'll share with you some truth that'll shatter your theories — or as I call it bullshit :) you may not like what I have to say so I need you focused, if you wouldn't mind.

I typed a response.

> I'm not sure why you've taken such an interest in teaching me but I'll make the time right now, as it seems you are, as well. Just give me a couple minutes to say bye to my girl and then I'm all yours...

I hit send and turned to JC, who was sitting upright, searching for something in her bag.

Before I even had the time to tell her I'd catch her later, with her head still down, she said to me, "Hey, girl, I gotta go pick up the girls from ballet. Text me later, okay? I wanna know what this dude has to say! After all, we did help you figure out who this Mr. Passion is." She winked at me and got up from her chair. "Thanks for the lunch, babe, and good luck!"

I didn't even watch to see her turn and give a quick wave as every fiber of my being was pulled back to my phone like a magnet. This mystery man had my full attention.

My hands shaking, I called in to work and told my boss I had an emergency errand to run and wouldn't be back to the office today, which he was totally cool with. It helped to be an attractive, no-bullshit kind of woman around a male-dominated accounting firm. I opened my messages and typed back to Mr. Passion.

> Ok. I'm all yours, Mr. Passion. I've cleared up my schedule so please, enlighten me. I'm intrigued by all the "bullshit" you heard from me and my girls.

Little did I know I had opened Pandora's box. I had just invited this man to turn the world as I knew it completely upside down. I would never again see men the same way as I had for three decades.

> Okay cool. Make yourself comfortable in that sexy, tight, olive green dress you have on and kick off those black, red-bottomed pumps, please.

My jaw dropped to the floor. This man could see me, now all alone, and had probably been watching me this entire time! I looked around subtly to see if I recognized anyone I had been sitting only a few feet away from this past weekend, but no one in sight looked like he could possibly be my Mr. Passion.

This all made me slightly uncomfortable and I badly wished either JC or Brie hadn't left so soon. Then I remembered I was in a public place and there was very little he could do to me. I looked back down at my phone and typed my next message.

> Clearly you can see me right now. Where are you?

I hit send and immediately typed a second message. Why not keep the mystery alive?

> You know what? Never mind. I don't wanna know.

> I'm ready when you are, Passion. Fire away with your wisdom.

I hit send. I gently removed my shoes under the table. As I awaited his response, I decided to grab the drink clearly sent by my mystery man, and sat back in my seat, enjoying the lightheadedness from the cool liquid working its way into my bloodstream. I unfolded my legs so he could see I was comfortable in my position. Perhaps if he had the right view, he could see I had neglected to put panties on that morning as I dressed for work. My phone beeped.

> Here it goes. You ladies believe a good man is anyone who talks a good game to you, a man with confidence who talks shit. You three, each in your own way, mentioned this "bad boy" image that you're attracted to because it shows you he's not intimidated by you. As beautiful women, you all agreed that a man who approached you with a good line is desirable, as many guys don't know how to approach you at all.

As I read his text message, I couldn't help but to nod in agreement, as everything this man was saying was spot on. He was describing a confident man, all right! Another *beep*.

> Let me let you in on a little secret, if I may?

> There is no such thing as a "bad boy." Bad boys do not exist, period! That name you ladies give to a man who can talk shit is merely a title for a guy who does not know how to respect a woman.

> Men are either able to speak intelligently and respectfully, or they talk nonsense because they don't know what to say. Men with nothing to say are immature boys trying to act grown.

> You females take that smooth talk as some gift of gab and fall for it every time. In the end, once the tough "bad boy" act is over and the shit talking stops (usually right after he gets you in bed and fucks you for hardly enough time to even get you truly aroused), you ladies are left feeling empty and with only your theories to cover your naked ass that you just gave to the dude for damn near nothing.

Although this man had never actually met me before, he was describing my past "situationships" to a T. No man ever stepped to me with any real substance to make me stop and consider getting into a relationship, so they just kind of stayed at friends with benefits. Just as Passion described, no matter how bomb the sex, it was only a matter of time before the dude got bored, the flame extinguished and it'd be on to the next.

I waited with bated breath for the next text to come in, hoping there would be more. I was at a complete loss for a response.

Beep.

> Furthermore, and I hope I'm not upsetting you, women tend to get stuck on the exterior of a man and settle for what's on the surface. How much money he has, what type of car he drives, his height or how he's the life of the party.

> But that's not how to determine a real man at all. A man can have all the money in the world and have no clue what it takes to please a woman to the point that her pussy drips at just the thought of how good her man treats her.

> You made a comment the other night that your type of man is tall and sexy, great in bed, and able to go all night... definitely doesn't sound like you've truly experienced passion. Thus the reason I've been asking you all week if you've ever really felt passion. Still with me?

I stared at my phone for what could have been minutes for all I knew. As soon as I snapped back to reality, I realized I had allowed my legs to come slightly apart, and had sunk deeper into my chair, completely relaxed. *Beep*.

> I'll conclude with this... good men only seem hard to find because women are too busy looking for the wrong kind of attention from guys, falling all over men who barely notice the important things that matter to a woman.

> Check it out: you wore an all black, sleeveless dress with black lace around the bust that pushed your breasts up so you didn't need a bra.

Your deep chocolate, almost black hair was ironed straight and fell to the middle of your back. You wore Chanel No. 5 (my favorite), which I noticed when you walked by my table to use the ladies' room. The nails on both your hands and feet were colored a bright lavender and your peep-toe heels had you standing about 5'11" ...which makes me guess you're about 5'7" without them.

You had a bracelet on that you've probably had since you were younger, as it had multiple charms on it, which means you're sentimental and you love hard. You made sure out of the many rings you had on, that your left ring finger was bare, which shows me you're a hopeless romantic who believes strongly in tradition and you look forward to getting married one day.

You like your right ear to be played with because that is the ear you repeatedly touched all night. If I came up behind you right now and you let me put my tongue in that ear, your pussy juices would flow right out of you and onto the seat you're sitting on because you didn't bother putting on any panties this morning.

So he could definitely see up my dress. I blushed.

Beep.

> I could go on and on. But the point I'm trying to make is that most women are clueless as to what a good man looks like, smells like, feels like...

> If you give me the chance to show you the difference between the men you think you like and the man you should compare all other men to, I will ask you, the beautiful girl in the olive dress sitting by herself on the deck, biting her lip and now quickly sitting up and crossing her legs as she remembers someone is taking note of her every move and has confirmed she has nothing on under that dress and is likely dripping all over the seat underneath her: felt passion... have you really?

I sat there reading every word of this stranger's assessment of my conversation with the girls that night and found it hard to find my breath. Every single word he said was true. But damn, how could I have missed this man paying such close attention to me while he was so close to me that night?

I put my phone down and fixed my dress; it had ridden up my thighs slightly. I swept my hair behind my ears and reapplied my lipstick that I'm sure I had sucked off by now. I picked up my phone and read every word again, slowly, as if I'd missed something the first time. He could see me, and he likely could tell how badly he had turned me on.

I hit reply.

> Mr. Passion, first let me thank you for sharing this with me. If you don't mind, I would like to share it with my girls who just left. They were just as curious to the kind of bullshit you were calling on all of us :) and after all, it was with their encouragement that I even texted you back in the first place. I hope that's ok.

> Although what you have shared with me hits home in a lot of ways, it's hard to relate to because I don't have the experience. You're right on one thing though... and I'm shy to admit it. But you had my pussy throbbing as I realized how focused you were on me that night. I may have to throw this dress away 😬 😬

> Even right now, knowing you're somewhere near, watching me, giving me a total breakdown of what I had on the other night, I'm totally turned on. My pussy is soaking wet. I'm imagining your dick hard as hell right now watching me shift back and forth in my seat as I write this...

> If I want to know more, will you teach me firsthand? I want to know more about your passion.

Beep.

> Follow my instructions carefully as we go and I will prove to you that passion is not what you see but what you FEEL. Are you ready for me to give you your first assignment? Are you ready to learn passion, lady?

> Yes, please. I'm ready to follow all instructions. Entirely.

I had no clue what the fuck I was getting myself into. On one hand, this dude could be a complete stalker creep. On the other hand, he turned me on with just his words more than I had ever been turned on in my life. *Beep.*

> Okay. There's a door all the way in the back corner of the patio, the one that says Staff Only. It leads to a stairwell. Get up and go straight to that door. Open it and go inside. I want you to tell me what you smell. Stand in there for a minute or two, eyes closed, so you don't focus on where you are but on your sense of smell only.

> Now put your shoes back on, get up, and do as you're told. I'll be waiting for you to return. Go!

My heart skipped a beat. No one had ever spoken to me like that. It excited me. I put my phone on the table in front of me then reached down and slipped my pumps back on. I stood and fixed my dress then turned around to find the door I was commanded to go through. I made a beeline straight to the back of the patio and walked right to the Staff Only door, closing it behind me as I caught my breath on the other side. My heart was beating so fast at the thought of entering a place I was clearly not supposed to be. This dude was going to get me into trouble. I hated to admit to myself I liked it. A lot. I had a feeling I would be doing whatever this man told me to do.

I took a step forward away from the door and closed my eyes, a sweet aroma filling my nostrils. I breathed a deep breath through my nose, letting it stay there a few moments to gather the sweet smell in the air. I recognized it immediately as Cool Water cologne. The smell was so strong it must have been sprayed just seconds before; I would not be able to get it out of my memory any time soon. As I stood in the stairwell, breathing in the delicious cologne, my pussy throbbed again and grew increasingly wet.

My phone beeped in my hand with instructions to go back to my seat outside immediately. Reluctantly, I took one last breath and reached for the doorknob.

Upon my table stood a single red rose in a thin bottle of water with a note underneath it. I smiled and shook my head. Taking my seat, I moved the rose to the side so I could unfold the note.

Welcome to the beginning of shattering every theory and idea of what a good man looks, smells, and feels like, baby ... I promise not to disappoint. Cheers to no more bullshit! Xoxo

I turned and looked all around me to see who, what, where ... He was nowhere to be found. I was speechless.

After a few minutes, I decided to test the waters to see what would happen if I got up and left. My pussy was aching to be told what to do next, and after a few minutes of my phone not beeping, I grabbed the rose and smiled with excitement as I headed out the door.

As I got to my car, I got a text on my phone.

> Have a great rest of your day, beautiful. Will text you soon!

Two days went by. Friday night I was home alone when my phone beeped. I figured it was Brie or JC teasing the idea of another girls' night, or my mother checking in on me.

I was so wrong.

It was Passion.

I had tried to get the other day out of my mind and focus on my work for the past few days, but I just couldn't shake the feelings that flowed through my entire body that Wednesday afternoon. I was so nervous to read the text but too excited not to. Just seeing "Mr. Passion" appear on my screen made my heart leap into my throat (I still didn't know his name).

> Hi beautiful. Ready for your next instructions? Great :) I want you to put on a sexy, short dress and your highest heels and head toward the corner of 46th St and 7th Avenue. I will tell you the exact location when you get there. Be there at 9:30pm sharp and please do not be late. A good man hates to be kept waiting. See you soon.

I looked at the clock—it was already a few minutes after seven. I jumped up and stripped my clothes off on the way to the shower and hopped in. In case this man was going to have me hanging upside-down from the ceiling, I wanted to make sure I shaved any unwanted hair thoroughly. He mentioned a short dress after all, meaning he had plans for my legs ... hopefully.

I made it to 46th and 7th with ten minutes to spare and waited for the text with the exact location. My phone vibrated in my clutch and I took it out. It was him.

> A few doors down on 46th St, you will see a hotel on your right called The Muse. Walk inside and go past the front desk directly toward the red velvet curtains. Through them you will see a bar. At the far end of the bar your favorite drink will be waiting for you. I will be waiting for you as well.

"My favorite drink?" I thought. This man really thought of everything. I turned around and started walking down 46th Street toward the blue fluorescent sign for the hotel. The closer I got, the faster my breathing became and the quicker my heart raced. I was about to meet Mr. Passion in the flesh.

The doorman opened the door and bowed his head to me. I walked past the threshold into the sleek, swanky lobby. I walked past the front desk toward the velvet curtains in the back. Beyond the curtains was a dimly lit bar as he'd said, with several high-top tables and about twelve stools along the long bar. The bar itself was white marble, with all-white furniture and red lights illuminating the bottles in a triangle formation behind the bar. I continued to the end of the bar as instructed. Seeing no one else around, aside from a few couples enjoying the privacy of their own booths across the room, I sat down in front of what looked like a chilled, dirty martini with blue cheese-stuffed olives.

I hadn't been drinking martinis either time I had been watched by Mr. Passion; how the hell did he know dirty martinis were my favorite drink? I was thoroughly impressed. The bartender greeted me by name and presented the martini, confirming it was, in fact, the drink meant for me.

Underneath the glass was a note.

Please make yourself comfortable and read the following carefully. Tonight you will have a date with me, yet not see me. You will only be able to text me while I watch you and direct you. You cannot reveal what you will be taught tonight to anyone. You must follow all of my instructions to a T and if not, I will end the date and you will be free to go.

I looked around, slightly disappointed I would not be seeing Passion directly tonight. The bartender offered me a menu and told me my entire tab had already been taken care of, so I should feel free to order anything I desired. I thanked him and looked back down at my phone to type my response.

> Ok Passion. What do you want me to do next? Thank you for the drink, by the way.

> Cheers, gorgeous. I do not want you to do anything just yet, aside from tell me... what makes your pussy wet?

Shocked at how forward he was, I typed a cheeky response, knowing he was near.

> I can show you better than I can tell you!

He didn't take the bait.

After another martini and about fifteen minutes of texting enough naughty talk to get my pussy juices to seep through my G-string, I had a visitor. A handsome man about six-foot-one, who closely resembled a young Denzel Washington, approached me and asked if I was alone.

"Yes. Kind of. But not really."

He didn't seem bothered and pulled out the chair next to me and sat. Because I had no instructions from Passion, my new friend and I got to know each other. I found out he was in town on business and came down from his room to have a drink or two to unwind from a long day of shooting (he was a music video director).

Boy, this man was so smooth, and the shit that came out of his mouth was music to my ears. Like clockwork, Passion would chime in with questions to ask this man which only confirmed he could indeed see me. My pussy throbbed harder at every text I received.

I apologized to the man, who introduced himself as Amari, for being on my phone so much while he was speaking. I told him answering my phone was the "kind of" part of my answer to his question of if I was alone or not.

I told him I was on a sort of cyber date, and that I hoped I wasn't being too rude. I had no idea telling this man in front of me I was on a date with another man would turn up his energy for me. I wondered if seeing this man flirting so hard with me would finally pull Passion out of hiding, so I turned up the energy as well.

Amari responded well to my new level of energy for him, but it also made him try even harder to get me to come up to his hotel room with him. Although I was loving the energy, I expected Passion to stop him or come rescue me, to no avail.

At this point, Amari had moved his chair closer to mine, almost touching, so that my legs were open and on either side of his leg. We faced each other as he leaned in closer and closer to me until our faces were only about a foot away from each other's. I was getting so horny, and suspected this man was part of Passion's plan. I took my phone off the bar and shot him a quick text.

> What are we doing here? Are you trying to see if I'm going to fuck this dude or not? Because it's not gonna happen.

> Why not? Is this not the type of man you like? Tall, dark, and talking shit? The type who can get into your panties with his words and want to fuck you on sight? What's the problem?

> I didn't say you had to do anything. That's up to you. What I did say is you have to follow my instructions. So... do you want to kiss him? You allowed him to sit nearly on top of you... so??

I could not deny what Passion had picked up on about my body language. I had not stopped Amari from coming close to me at all. I texted a response.

> Yes, I'm attracted to him. And yes, I wanna kiss him, if I'm going to be honest with you.

> Then what are you waiting for?? Kiss him already and get it over with!

I frowned. I had not expected Passion to direct me to kiss this man, but I did want to, and I had to follow Passion's instructions, otherwise our fun would all be over. I looked up; Amari was looking directly into my eyes, searching, and hungry. I leaned in closer to feel his warm breath on my lips.

"Amari, I gotta be honest, I haven't been paying attention to a word you've been saying. All I can think about is how badly I want you to kiss me."

At those words, he smiled a devilish grin and leaned his face closer to mine, his bottom lip barely touching mine. He lingered there for a moment, knowing he was driving me absolutely insane, and then reached his hand behind my neck and pulled me closer, shoving his tongue deep into my mouth. With this single gesture my juices puddled up all over the chair beneath me. I closed my eyes and for just a moment, allowed myself to pretend this was Passion kissing me.

Something stopped me from allowing myself to live in that fantasy world for long, something missing.

His cologne. The cologne. This man did not smell like Cool Water, and that memory of the scent snapped me back to reality.

Passion or not, this man could kiss his ass off, our tongues effortlessly twisting around each other like the perfect dance. Thinking about Passion reminded me he was obviously somewhere close, watching my every move. I was going to make sure I gave him the show he wanted.

I pulled slightly away from Amari and opened my eyes, staring at him intently, making sure he knew what I was asking for next. I took his bottom lip in my mouth and sucked on it gently, running my tongue from one side of his lip to the other before sticking my tongue all the way into his mouth as I arched my back. Very slowly, he ran his hand all the way up my bare thigh and underneath the hem of my dress. With his other hand he shifted my chair to get a better angle as his hand rubbed on my clit over my panties. He moaned deeply into my mouth as he felt how wet he had made me over the last half hour or so of talking shit to me. With his index finger, he pulled at my G-string and moved it to the side as he played with my pussy, spreading my wetness all over me.

Beep. Passion! Just as Amari was about to put his fingers inside me, I pulled away from him and opened my eyes, trying to locate my phone like I had just awakened from a deep sleep. With one hand still caressing my pussy, Amari handed me my phone with his other hand. I opened the message.

> Take your panties off and put them in his jacket pocket. Move to the very end of the bar where you will be less conspicuous. Let's not get you kicked out of here before the fun begins ;) Once you get there, sit back down and open your pussy so he can work his long fingers all the way inside. Go now.

Shocked again. I slid Amari's hand out from between my legs as I stood up and pulled my dress down.

"Follow me," I whispered into Amari's ear before running my tongue along the edge and sucking gently on his earlobe. I led him to the end of the bar, where I directed him to sit. I stood in front of him and inched my panties down underneath my dress so I could subtlety pull them all the way down. I stepped each stiletto out of them and grabbed them off the floor. I reached for his jacket and put my black G-string in his pocket, as instructed by Passion.

The feeling this all gave me was such a rush! The oddest part was that although I had my own level of confidence, this was nothing I would have done on my own. Yet it all felt so natural to me. I took Passion's instructions, and turned them way up to make them my own. Something about impressing this man I had not even met yet turned me on so much more than even what I was physically being commanded to do. I found myself turned on by both men for two totally different reasons.

There was a lesson there beyond sexuality that Passion was teaching me, something I still could not quite put my finger on. The thought of these two men, working together on me to make me cum was nearly enough to send me over the edge.

Amari's fingers found my G-spot. He massaged it deeper and slower as I moved my hips to meet his fingers in tandem. I grew closer and closer to orgasm. I moved in to kiss him so I could cum all over his hand as his mouth muffled my deep moans. Then I let myself go.

As soon as I could catch my breath, my phone beeped.

> Are you done cumming all over his hands? Please get yourself together and excuse yourself. If you noticed before you went through the velvet curtains, there are bathrooms just beyond the front desk. I want you to gather your things and head there alone. Go into the third stall to your left. Close the door behind you but don't lock it and wait there with your back to the door. Go.

I looked up at Amari and he looked back at me as if he knew what I was about to say. He kissed me softly, smiled, and without me saying a word, he whispered, "Go, baby." I cocked my head and gave him a confused smile.

"Excuse me. I'm not sure if I'll be back, so if not, it was great to meet you, Amari." I smoothed down my dress, grabbed my clutch, and headed back through the red curtains as quickly as I could in my heels.

I hurried through the lobby toward the bathroom, fearing I might squirt all over the black marble floors from the friction of my pussy lips rubbing together from Amari's fingers being deep inside me.

I pushed open the door to the restroom to find several elegant crystal sinks and floor-to-ceiling mirrors all around me. There were six or seven doors, all with different words written in black font against the smoked out, opaque glass doors. A single glass chandelier hung from the middle of the ceiling with hundreds of individual lights, creating a romantic, dimly lit hue.

As I was standing there admiring the detail of the bathroom, my phone beeped with another instruction.

> In the third stall, you will see something hanging from the light on the back wall. I want you to pull your hair back in a ponytail and put the object on. With your back to the door, put your hands on the wall in front of you like you're about to be patted down. Oh, and don't you dare wash any of your pussy juices off until I tell you to!

I located the third door on the left and cautiously pushed the door open, bracing myself for what Passion might have set up inside. The light inside burned a hot, red glow, which made everything, including the white porcelain toilet, appear red. The scent of Cool Water cologne immediately filled my nostrils and my pussy throbbed. There didn't seem to be anything out of the ordinary, except a black cloth hanging from the light.

I closed the door behind me, instinctively reaching to lock it, but remembering I had been instructed against doing so, and noticed the enormity of the floor-to-ceiling door. This place was absolutely breathtaking. I reached in front of me and gently lifted the cloth off the light. It was a silk blindfold. I smiled and shook my head again. I already had such a fondness for this mystery man of mine.

I tied the blindfold around my wrist and reached into my purse for a hair tie. I hung my purse on the hook behind me and faced the back wall, then tied my hair into a ponytail. I put the blindfold on, reached out in front of me to put my hands on the wall and waited.

My heart raced as I realized the blindfold was the source of the cologne, and the scent entirely consumed me. Every small sound I heard made my heart skip a beat; I was hypersensitive to all other senses without my sight.

The door opened behind me. I knew right away it was Passion from the second wave of Cool Water that overtook the small washroom we now shared. My heart was about to beat right out of my chest. The door closed and I heard the door lock. I bit my lip in anticipation.

"Mr. Passion, is that you?"

I felt completely vulnerable. I was blindfolded, arms reaching out high above my head on the wall in front of me, and in a locked bathroom stall with a stranger who might be considered by some standards a total creep.

Mr. Passion

"Who else would it be?" I said with a suggestive ring to my voice. A shiver ran up her spine as she heard my voice, which turned me on more than watching her getting finger fucked. Without even needing to touch her, I knew her pussy was the wettest right now that it had been all night. As she stood there in her heels, blindfolded, pussy lips exposed and yearning for my touch, I whispered in her ear everything that had happened to her tonight on our cyber date.

"I have stayed at this hotel many times and know it well. On the other side of the red curtains are the elevators, and there's a glass door that is very hard to see from where you sat. I could see you from the moment you walked in with a confidence I hadn't yet seen in you. Amari is a friend of mine who I asked to approach you, knowing he would drive you crazy and be able to talk the shit to you that you say you like so much, just to show you that guys like him are just that ... shit talkers. Like many guys, he didn't care when you told him you were on a cyber date with another man because his only focus was trying to fuck you. And admit it, you wanted to fuck him, too, didn't you?"

"I did," she responded meekly.

"Say it, baby. You wanted to fuck Amari," I demanded, raising the volume of my voice slightly.

"I did. I wanted to fuck Amari."

"And you liked how wet he made your pussy, didn't you? Say it."

"I loved how wet he made my pussy."

I reached around and put her panties against her nose.

"I want you to take a deep breath in and smell how good your pussy smells and smell what Amari did to you for me."

She took an audible breath in, letting out a gentle moan as she exhaled.

"The Cool Water cologne you smelled the other day was purposefully used to let you know it is not how a man looks, but how well he pays attention to the woman he desires that makes him superior. On the first night I saw you, you complimented a man who wears the same cologne as I do, Cool Water. Anything less than full attention to detail only means a man is not worth what he claims."

Sarah

As he talked, he got closer and closer to me until his hands were gripping my waist, touching me for the first time. Chills ran up and down my entire body. Goosebumps erupted over the surface of my skin. His touch was enough to make my pussy gush, and my juices dripped down the inside of my thigh.

His breath was hot on my right ear, the one he knew was my weak spot, as he whispered slowly, "So ... You think you've felt passion?"

All I could do is melt into him. I leaned my head back into his neck and his cologne filled my head once again. He nibbled on my ear, which almost made me lose my legs underneath me.

"I'm going to taste all that Amari did to you now." He backed away from my body and got on his knees.

Mr. Passion

I gave her ear one last nibble and then got down on my knees behind her. Starting at her ankles, I ran my hands up the outsides of her calves. She had the smoothest skin I had ever felt. Once I reached her knees I moved to the inside of her thighs, gently nudging her legs to open wider so I could have fuller access to her dripping pussy. She spread her legs wider as I continued to caress her inner thighs. She arched her back to my touch, giving me better access to lick the cum off her leg.

I put my right hand on her lower back and she relaxed under my touch. Her torso sank closer to the floor as I ran my tongue up from underneath and onto her ass. With both hands,

I gripped her ass and spread her cheeks. I stuck my tongue out as far as I could to reach her clit. I lapped up and down like a dog that hadn't had a drink of water in days as I swallowed down all the juices Amari had prompted.

She reached behind my head and pulled me closer in, immersing my entire face deep into her pussy as I stuck my tongue inside her. As I fucked her pussy with my tongue, she begged for me not to stop, her breathing getting heavier and heavier with every stroke. I didn't stop until she came all over my face.

Sarah

This man was eating my pussy like a bear trying to get honey out of a beehive after he knocked it down from the tree. I was all about it, and the more I thought about it, the more I became restless with the fact this man had made me wait so long to feel his touch, his tongue, his presence. The nerve! I wanted badly to get even, but of course to my benefit. I reached behind me to grab the back of his neck and pushed his head hard against me, driving his face deeper into my pussy.

I reached my climax, and after cumming all over his face I couldn't deny it any longer: I needed to feel this man inside me.

I groped for his collar, grabbed it, and yanked him to his feet. As he found his bearings behind me, I reached back and found his belt, undid it and let his pants fall to the floor. His hard dick was sticking straight out. I grabbed his throbbing cock in my hand as I arched my back. With my right hand at the base, I spread my pussy lips open with my left. I guided his rock hard dick against the flesh of my pussy, and braced for impact. I could barely stand not having him inside me any longer, the tip of his dick teasing the opening of my pussy. With my hand, I shoved him deep inside my pussy walls as hard as I could, encouraging him to fuck the shit out of me.

I was so fucking horny at this point that soft lovemaking was way out of the question. I begged him not to show any mercy. He immediately took the not-so-obvious hint and ravaged my pussy so much I could feel my walls swelling aggressively around his dick. I lost track of whether it was his dick swelling as he pounded me, or if it was my walls inflaming from the rapid thrusting going on inside of me. Either way, it didn't matter, because Amari had done a wonderful job of preparing me for the complete onslaught of this perfect stranger behind me.

At that moment I was all in with Passion; no matter what he demanded of me, I would fulfill to his expectations and beyond. I desperately wanted Passion to know not only could I take on his challenges, but I could also handle his relentless deep pussy pounding against the best of them.

Mr. Passion

Sarah still wore the silk blindfold and had not yet gotten a glimpse of me. I wanted her first sight of me to be of me pleasing her, the way it should be. I wanted her to see exactly how it would be if she chose to accept my final instruction.

I pulled out of her and spun her around. I steadied her on her heels before dropping back down to my knees in front of her.

"Hold the walls for balance if you need to." I grabbed her behind the knee and slowly guided her thigh to rest on my shoulder. I spread her pussy wide open and slid my fingers inside her. She moaned softly. As I fucked her pussy with my fingers I told her to take her blindfold off. I moved my face closer to her clit and flicked it with my tongue. For the first time ever, we made eye contact.

Sarah

I removed my blindfold and took my first look at Mr. Passion. He was face deep in my soaking wet pussy and looked like the most delicious man I had ever laid my eyes on.

As I headed toward my climax once again, I noticed, for the first time, the letters inscribed on the outside of the door, backward from my view: the letters P.A.S.S.I.O.N. I giggled at the irony and crept toward the edge of climax with this man's tongue in my pussy.

This man, who I called Passion, had just taught me how to feel it. How to feel passion; both literally and figuratively, for the first time in my life. He had single handedly laid many of my theories of men to rest by sucking and fucking them right out of me in the proper way.

After I came for the billionth time in the bathroom of passion, my mystery man stood up and introduced himself.

"Baby girl, I'm Sean. My final instruction, should you comply, is for you to allow me to make you my girlfriend."

"Right now?" I asked, stunned. He began to laugh and I realized how silly my question was.

"Yes, Sarah. I know what I want and I don't see any reason to wait to have it. Will you accept my final instruction for the evening?"

It shouldn't have surprised me that this man who knew so much about me also knew my name. But still, to hear it from his lips rendered me speechless.

One thing was for sure, Passion had completely crushed every theory I had of what a good man was, and exceeded every expectation of what a real man is. He was everything I didn't even know I wanted. I was hooked, and there was no way I was going to refuse to follow his instructions now.

"Of course I will accept."

He took my face in his hands and kissed my lips for the first time. All I could taste was passion.

Swingin' Bi

Noah

My girl Blair and I were coming up on our first Valentine's Day together as husband and wife, and I wanted to do something memorable for her. In our marriage vows, we agreed that we would always keep our relationship "fresh and new."

Early on in our courtship, we discovered that we brought out a special freakiness in each other, and made sure to vow, in front of all of our loved ones, that we would never lose sight of that; after all, it was the trust and honesty we developed through our freaky experiences together that sealed our bond and always kept us coming back for more. As expected, that promise went over the heads of most of our guests.

I wanted to remind Blair that I had not forgotten those vows. What better way to show my wife I loved her than by honoring our marriage vows? I knew the perfect gift that we could share with each other, and a much better "date night" than going out to eat like we did regularly.

I researched online and found the best swingers club within 100 miles. The place was called SILK and it was only about a thirty-five-minute drive, which would give us ample time to discuss our expectations and boundaries. We had never been to a swingers spot before, and although we'd had a few threesomes, I knew they would not compare to a sexual smorgasbord. We would have a whole menu of people to choose from, ready to fuck for us. And because it was Valentine's Day, I figured only the biggest freaks would be out at a swingers spot, spreading the "love!"

I woke Blair up with breakfast in bed on Valentine's Day morning: scrambled eggs and strawberry waffles, her all-time favorite. I brought her both ice water and orange juice, and a single red rose in a tiny vase. As she ate, I went into the other room to retrieve the gift that I picked out for her, as well as the Valentine's Day card that I bought.

Blair

A warm sensation pressed against my forehead, and as consciousness filled my body, I realized it was Noah kissing me before my eyes even opened. I had almost forgotten what day it was. A week ago, he made me promise I would allow him to plan our entire Valentine's Day. He pleaded that if he had to submit to my every wish next year, then so be it, but he wanted to claim this year.

I reluctantly agreed last week, but now, as my sleepy eyes opened to the sight of my favorite breakfast, I silently celebrated that decision. The silver tray Noah set up for me was covered in red rose petals, and a single red rose accompanied the eggs and strawberry waffles.

Before I could even muster a "Good morning, baby" or a "Happy Valentine's Day," Noah glided out of the room. I could tell he was up to something, because he was even less of a morning person than I was.

He came back with a thin, red, rectangular box with a gold ribbon tied neatly in a bow on top of it. A card in a pink envelope with "For my Wife" written beautifully in script accompanied it. My smile grew wider as he handed me the box.

"Happy first Valentine's Day, my queen. Open the card first."

I loved the sight of him so excited.

From the very beginning of our relationship, he was most excited when doing something for me or when making me happy. Pleasing each other in every way brought both of us the most joy.

"Happy first Valentine's Day, my king," I responded.

I placed the box on the bed next to me. He handed me the card and I took it in both hands, admiring the letters in metallic gold ink. It was breathtaking, and I could tell Noah had it done somewhere. I gently lifted the adhesive flap of the envelope and removed the card from inside. As I read the message Noah had written, he came and sat down next to me in anticipation as I read the inscription:

To my beautiful wife on our first Valentine's Day as a married couple:

I never want you to forget how much I love you and cherish you. On the day we committed our lives to each other, we vowed to always keep our relationship fresh and interesting, and on this first Valentine's Day, I have planned an evening that we will forever remember together. Cheers to our love and to a lifetime full of growth and excitement! Happy Valentine's Day, my queen.

Love,

Your husband

P.S. You're not allowed to open the box until I tell you to! No exceptions, lady!

Noah

I sat next to Blair as she read my card, waiting until she reached the end and anticipating the mini hissy fit I knew she would throw when she realized she could not open the box just yet. I had never met another person that loved surprises as much as her, so the fuss would all just be an act to show me how excited she was.

She slowly reached for her breakfast tray without saying a word and placed it on the nightstand nearest her. As she turned back to face me, her mouth twisted into an ear-to-ear smile. Suddenly, she threw the card off the side of the bed, pushed me onto my back, climbed on top of me and began play fighting me, begging to let her open her gift. She tried to pull a fast one on me by pinning my hands above my head so she could reach for the box, but I saw what she was trying to do from a mile away and flipped her over so that she was face down on the bed.

I sat on top of her, pushing the box onto the floor and out of reach. Blair squealed. I grabbed the nearest pillow and buried her head in it as I got off of her and stood up, grabbing the box as I went. She got up and stood on the bed, looking down at me, and with her eyes and devilish smile, silently threatened to jump on me. I dropped the box again just in time to catch her as she wrapped her arms and legs around me and kissed me hard. I kissed her back, matching her passion, as I stood holding her for several minutes.

Eventually, I took the few steps toward the bed and laid her down on her back, her legs still wrapped tightly around my waist. When she gyrated her hips up against mine, I pushed away from her and then smacked her hard on the ass.

"Finish eating," I commanded.

She rolled her eyes and threw her head back in dramatic dissatisfaction and I got up, laughing and stealing a bite of eggs. She sat up and I set her breakfast in front of her, leaning in and kissing her again before I whispered, "Happy Valentine's Day, my love."

She rolled her eyes again and in a snarky tone, pretending to still be upset, she replied, "I love you too, jerk!" She smiled my favorite huge smile of hers and picked up her fork to continue eating. "You at least have to let me keep the box in my possession. I swear I won't open it until you tell me to."

I bent down, picked the box up once more, tossed it onto the bed next to her and then turned to leave the room.

"Thank you!" she shouted after me. As I got to the end of the long hallway, she added, "I love you, baby!"

We spent most of the day in bed, just relaxing and enjoying each other's company. I was relieved when it seemed as though Blair had forgotten about the gift. I knew she hadn't, of course, but at least she stopped whining about it. I knew it would be worth the wait for the purpose the gift served and would heighten her anticipation that much more for what I had planned later. At dinnertime, Blair prepared my favorite meal for us, pepper steak with roasted potatoes and green beans. Damn, could this woman cook!

After dinner, she ran to the bedroom and came back to the table with a large wrapped frame in her arms along with a card. I tore off the paper from around the frame to reveal a large portrait Blair had drawn of us. It was the first photo we had ever taken together and the thoughtfulness of her gift brought me close to tears. I had no idea that Blair could draw so well. My dick got hard at the thought of what other talents my wife had that I had yet to discover.

I stood up and pulled her into me, grabbing her ass with both my hands. She reached for the back of my neck and kissed me hard, shoving her whole tongue in my mouth. Making me emotional as well as cooking for me always made her happy and horny. Grabbing her ass harder with my left hand, I slid my right hand in between her legs as I pulled her up closer to me and grabbed her pussy from the back, massaging it over her jeans. She let a deep moan escape her mouth and into mine, letting me know exactly the effect the move had on her. She ran her nails down my back, just hard enough to send a shiver down my spine. My dick grew harder.

I could begin to feel the moisture seeping through her jeans as I had both my hands now rubbing her pussy, lifting her onto her tippy toes for fuller access. She wrapped one arm around my shoulder for support, and with her other hand she massaged my hard dick over my pants.

I told her to hold on as I lifted her up by her ass and wrapped her legs around me. I carried her around to the empty side of the table and laid her down on her back. As I stood in between her legs, I grabbed both her ankles and placed each foot on the table. I undid the button of her jeans and pulled down her zipper. She lifted her ass so I could slide her jeans off and her bright pink thong down with it and discarded both on the floor at my feet.

I planted tiny kisses from her left knee up her inner thigh and back down her right thigh to her other knee. I ran my tongue down the entirety of her thigh as she spread her legs open so I could flick her clit gently with my tongue before I headed back down her other thigh. I grabbed both of her knees, spreading her legs even further and spreading her pussy wide open in front of me. I leaned down and with her pussy in my face, I spat on it before putting my whole face in it, licking relentlessly up and down on her clit. She arched her back and moaned as I drove my tongue directly into her pussy, sticking my tongue in as far as I could and fucking her with my tongue. I took it out and licked her from her pussy opening up to her clit and back down again, over and over until her juices covered my face.

This was the first step in what I had planned for her tonight; getting her completely horny and wanting more. I licked her and fucked her pussy with my tongue until she screamed out and squirted all in my mouth, calling out my name as she came. Just as she thought I was about to give her the pounding she was craving, I lifted her to a seated position, bare ass on our dining room table, wiped my mouth, and told her to get in the shower. I instructed her to shave herself completely bald and when she was done she could open the box. This of course got her all excited as she hopped up, kissed me deeply on the mouth, and skipped out of the room. I loved how childlike she became after a good orgasm, and my dick throbbed knowing what type of night we were in for.

Blair

After we finished eating dinner, Noah made me his dessert right on the dining room table. I loved when he took my body anywhere he pleased.

He promised after a shower I could finally open the gift he got me. I ran to the master bathroom, leaving a trail of the rest of my clothes behind me as I went. I ran myself a hot shower, making sure I shaved myself silky smooth all over. When I stepped out, I saw the red box with its gold bow placed next to the sink with another smaller card sitting on top. This one had no envelope, and was just a card folded in half like a tent. I grabbed the card and turned it upright. Inside were instructions.

Baby,

From here on out, I will need you to follow my every instruction. Open the box and put on what's inside. Do what it is you do that makes you smell so damn good all the time and put on a tight little dress of your choice. I need you to be ready by 10:00 p.m. sharp. Don't keep your husband waiting.

-N

I tossed the card on the countertop and grabbed the box, untying the ribbon with ease. I removed the top and the white tissue paper inside to unveil a sexy, red and black lace lingerie set with matching red panties, garter belt and black thigh-high stockings. How was I not surprised that my man would want me decked out in the sexiest lingerie on our first Valentine's Day?

I took my time rubbing down my entire body with my Vicki's shea oil, and then sprayed my signature body spray all over me. I put on the red panties and bra first, then slid over my hips the body suit with attached garter belt. When everything was in place, I slipped on the thigh-highs and secured them to the clasps on the garter belt. I stood in front of the full-length mirror and admired my gift. I had never seen a more beautiful lingerie set, and I honestly never felt so sexy in my life.

I blew out my hair and grabbed my makeup bag. I wanted to keep my makeup simple, as my outfit promised to grab enough attention. I applied a thin layer of foundation, emphasized my brows and curled my lashes. I applied mascara and threw on a layer of nude gloss. Normally, I would have opted for a red lip on Valentine's Day, but I knew Noah would end up being the one who wore it if I put it on.

I took a final close-up look at my face in the mirror before I headed into the bedroom toward the walk-in closet. I chose a dress that was short enough so that the garter straps and the top of my thigh highs were visible. I figured why not let people see what I was working with? Noah wouldn't have wanted the gift to go unappreciated by everyone who laid their eyes on me, right?

I couldn't have been more correct. After choosing my red-bottomed black patent leather Louis Vuittons, I headed downstairs to where Noah was, on the phone, pacing the living room. Once he turned around and noticed me standing there, he quickly ended his call, barely able to speak. I gave him a sly smile as he dropped his phone on the couch and walked toward me.

"How do I look?" I asked, faking schoolgirl timidity.

"You look good enough to eat, baby. You're begging me to take you on the dining room table again with that dress ..."

I gave him a big smile as he stood in front of me. I stood on my tippy toes and looked up to kiss him gently on the mouth.

"I'm ready for my next instruction, sir," I said.

"Get your sexy ass in the car!" He smacked my bottom.

I had absolutely no clue where we were going, but Noah got on the highway and headed north. About ten minutes into the drive, while we were talking about how mild the night was for mid-February, he slipped his hand onto my thigh under my garter strap and switched subjects.

"You ready to know where we're headed?"

I turned my whole body toward him as I shifted in my seat, which unintentionally allowed his fingertips to graze the top of my pussy over my panties.

"Yes, baby! God, I thought you'd never tell me!" I exclaimed, a little more excited than I had intended as his fingers rubbed between my legs.

He smiled his beautiful smile at me, pulled his hand away and grabbed something from the back seat. He handed me his iPad with a webpage open and told me my last instruction for the night was to review what was on the page and to tell me what I thought. As I stared at the glowing page, I read across the top of the screen the word "SILK." As I scrolled down the page, I realized we were on our way to our first swingers club together, and immediately my pussy began to throb. I looked over at Noah, who was looking at the road, and just stared at him until I got his attention. When he finally glanced over at me I gave him a devilish look.

"Baby, are you serious? We're really going to this place?"

"Is that okay with you?" His voice and face both showed concern.

"Okay?! Baby, this has secretly been on my bucket list of things to do together since forever!"

His shoulders relaxed. "Beat ya to it, babygirl." He smiled at me and winked, then turned back to the road. "Look it over so you can get an idea of what the place is like. It's the best swingers spot within 100 miles of us. We got about a half hour until we're there."

As I scrolled through the pages of the site, I landed on the FAQs page, which was the most helpful. I had so many questions, as I had never been to a swingers spot before. What will the people be like? Can you fuck anywhere or are there special rooms for that? Is group sex allowed? Will there be single ladies or do you need a man to enter? Will there be single men?

I found most of my answers on the site; the rest I knew Noah and I would find out together. Neither of us had ever been to a swingers club, and so we were both surely in for a treat.

He interrupted my search. "Is there anything in particular that you'd like to try tonight?"

I looked over at him, a bit overwhelmed at the range of possible ways to answer his loaded question. My mind raced at the prospect of fucking in front of a bunch of strangers.

"It's always been a fantasy of mine to have people watch me have sex," I admitted.

"I can help you out with that," he promised, his fingers gently caressing my inner thighs. "You've always liked being watched, huh?"

"Always. There's something sexy to me about turning people on by being turned on. I don't just want to be watched, I want other people to want to fuck just by looking at me. And then I want them to fuck."

"Everywhere we go people want to fuck just by looking at you. I'm excited to see them actually do it. What else?"

"I want to stay with you the whole night. I think a great rule would be that we always play together," I added.

"I agree. If one of us says no, it's a no for both of us. We come first."

"Pun intended." I smiled over at Noah, who was already smiling at me. We both laughed.

"Okay … and what about things you aren't comfortable with? Any hard boundaries?"

"Not really. Just that we stick together. I think we should just play it by ear and see what finds us. As long as we're together, I think I'm okay with everything."

"Okay. Let's have a safe word, that way if either of us is uncomfortable we can let the other one know. How about we ask the other one the question, 'Remember that time in Vegas?' and that'll be our cue to shut it down."

I tried to picture a scene in which I might find myself uncomfortable and if I could see myself asking that question. It seemed cryptic enough and relevant, and also had a hint of warning to it, which I liked.

"I like it. It's soft though, like a warning. How about that question is our yellow light. I'm comfortable with a hard, '*Stop*,' being our word to shut things down."

"Okay then. 'Stop' or 'no,' whichever is more appropriate, no matter how into it the other one is."

"Deal," I concluded as Noah parked the car. We had arrived at our destination.

He got out of the car and came around to open my door for me. He reached for my hand and helped me out, pulling me in close before closing the door behind me.

"Happy Valentine's Day, baby. Let's go get 'em." He cupped my face in his hands and kissed me softly, careful not to mess up my makeup so early in the night.

"Happy Valentine's Day, my love." I smiled a devilish grin. "Let's raise hell."

Once we were inside the front door, two drop-dead gorgeous women greeted us from behind a glass counter. The one on the left was tall and slim, with a short, fire-red wig on, neatly cropped into a bob. She had on a matching red see-through lace catsuit that slightly showed her nipples through the front, with a deep plunging neckline that went past her bellybutton. Her lips were adorned with bright red lipstick that made her teeth look a brilliant white when she smiled.

The brunette on the right was slightly shorter and had curves that never ended. Her nice, perky, DD tits were covered only with black pasties in the shape of X's to hide her nipples. She had a tiny waist, flat stomach, and a big, tight ass with her cheeks busting out of the bottom of her little denim shorts. The button was undone and her zipper down with the hem folded over led the eyes right down toward her black G-string that peeked out, the straps sitting high above on her hips. Her body looked like it was straight out of a fitness magazine, and her piercing green eyes could burn a hole right through you.

Noah

Blair admired the two bombshells while I paid the entrance fee and checked in our bottle of Grey Goose. I had read on their website while doing my research that this place didn't serve any alcohol, but was BYOB instead. After following instructions to read the "Rules of Engagement," which were handwritten in ink that illuminated brightly under a UV black light on the wall, we were ready to enter the club.

The brunette with the banging body led us through a black silk curtain into the main dance room and brought our bottle to the bar, where she explained we only had to tell the bartender the last name and given number associated with our bottle to get a drink. She then offered us a tour of the place, which we politely declined, and then walked away, leaving us to our own devices. Blair and I both stared at this chick as she walked away, imagining exactly what we would do to her.

We ordered our first round of drinks and decided to check the place out. We walked to the end of the bar where there was another silk curtain, this one halfway drawn. Blair peeked her head inside first, then looked back over her shoulder at me with a huge grin on her face. She raised her eyebrows and gave me a tiny nod, letting me know she wanted me to follow her inside.

Beyond the curtain we found eight or so private spaces, entirely enclosed with silk curtains, each just large enough to fit a queen-sized bed with lots of plush pillows. Each space was designed in a different style, half of them already with curtains drawn. We heard soft moans coming from behind the curtains, and Blair looked up at me as we laughed in unison. There was one huge, round, crimson red ottoman in the center of the room, and the lights were dimmed. Another set of black silk curtains hung at the opposite end of the room, marking an exit.

We took it all in as we crossed the room, trying to see what we could peek at through closed curtains. One couple, either intentionally or not, hadn't closed their curtains all the way and we subtly peeked inside, making sure to keep a safe distance to not disturb the doggy-style pairing. As we got closer, we realized how the decor worked to muffle sound as this woman, bare ass in the air getting pounded and slapped mercilessly, was not at all holding back her screaming and moaning.

As we watched this scene together, Blair's plump ass backed up ever so slightly onto my already hard dick. She grabbed my hands that were limp by my sides and placed them on each of her tits, her hands on top of mine. I stepped forward so her body was against mine and we watched live sex for the first time together.

She rubbed her ass against my dick and I slid my hands down her sides and onto her hips, leading her forward as I walked closely behind her toward the black silk curtains. She was clearly turned on; we both were, but I knew if she rubbed against me for much longer I'd pull her onto the nearest bed and fuck her right then and there.

We went through the black curtain, entering a smaller room with a few couches and small ottomans and end tables. Along one opaque, black glass wall were five or six doors, barely noticeable unless opened a crack. The wall itself did not go all the way up to the ceiling; instead, it stopped about a foot short, exposing the top of each anteroom to the room we stood in now. There was only one other couple in the room, making out on one of the couches. It was clearly too early for this room yet, as we heard no noise coming from any of the anterooms. We continued to walk through and located the locker rooms; we figured these would come in handy later in the evening.

We were finished with our drinks and decided to go for a refill and dance a little. On the dance floor, four raised podiums featured stripper poles going up to the high ceiling. The room was one giant circle, and the wall opposite the rounded bar was lined completely with elevated couches that you needed to climb three stairs to get to, allowing you to see all the action with a better view. I grabbed Blair and pulled her onto the dance floor, this time ready for her to rub her ass all over me. After a few minutes of bumping and grinding, Blair turned around in my arms and stood on tippy toes to whisper something in my ear.

Blair

I had never seen a dick so big in my entire life. I mean, I had a serious Mandingo fetish when it came to porn, but I had never witnessed one like this in the flesh. Just a few yards from where Noah and I were dirty dancing, a curvy but petite Latina shaped like a coke bottle, still completely clothed, was sitting against the edge of one of the stripper pole stages, taking all the way down her throat the massive dick of the dude standing in front of her, fucking her face on the dance floor.

It took me completely by surprise—I had forgotten we were in a swingers club with all the dancing going on around us. It immediately turned me on to see, but a part of me couldn't help but feel like what they were doing was taboo. I spun around in Noah's arms to check if he was seeing what I was, but he seemed clueless to his surroundings as well, completely consumed with my ass throwing it back on his seriously hard dick.

"Look, baby!" I urged, as I nodded in the direction of the public blowjob happening right in front of us.

"Damn, that dude is packin'!" he responded.

Now, my man isn't into guys or anything, but he does know how to pay a compliment where a compliment is due.

"How does that make you feel, baby?" he asked me, pulling me into him closer so I could feel his dick against my thigh.

"Honestly, I wasn't expecting that, but my pussy is throbbing sooo ..." I trailed off suggestively. "How the hell is she fitting that whole thing in her mouth? They have no shame!" We both fell into a fit of giggles.

I became completely mesmerized by this couple, in front of everyone to watch, as this chick took her man all the way down her throat, gagging and spitting on his dick in the middle of the dance floor as if no one was around. After a few minutes of dancing and watching I became so turned on that I grabbed Noah's hand and led him to the back where the lockers were. Enough people had disappeared off the dance floor and I wanted to find out where the next action was happening.

We decided to head toward the room adjacent to the locker rooms with all the anterooms to see if they were yet in use. We noticed everyone was walking around in white robes. We had entered phase two of the night, where clothes were optional.

We decided to follow suit and each headed into our respective locker rooms to change. I decided to keep on my heels, thigh highs, and garter belt so Noah could further enjoy the gift he gave me.

We met each other in the main room, adorned in our own white cotton robes. One couple was clearly getting busy in one of the private rooms, as the chick was screaming her head off in what sounded like both pleasure and pain.

From our view walking out of the locker rooms, we noticed a window we hadn't seen before. We looked at each other and with a smile and nod, silently agreed to check it out together.

A door opened next to the window and a couple walked out, smiling and glowing and glistening. As we approached the window, we saw a little sign next to the door that simply stated, "COUPLES ONLY." We looked at each other. Smiling, Noah seductively asked, "Shall we?"

I peered into the window and saw a giant room, the entire floor one large elevated mattress with only a small walkway from the door leading to the back of the room. I smiled back at him. "Looks like my personal fantasy room."

He opened the door for me and I walked in, shy at first. He closed the door behind him and put his hands on my hips as he led me further into the room. There were about twenty couples in the room, and hardly anyone had their robes on. Sex was happening all around us. Girls going down on guys, guys going down on girls; there were even two girls sixty-nining as their men watched. Doggy style, missionary, guys pinning their girls up against the wall as they fucked them silly ...

I was taking it all in as we walked further and further into the room when suddenly, Noah grabbed me firmly and turned me to face the mattress, putting his hand on the back of my neck and pushing me slightly forward so that my ass and pussy lips were exposed from under my super short robe. He stood behind me as I allowed my hands to catch myself on the bed in front of me. With one hand still on the back of my neck, he slid his other hand under my ass and grabbed my whole pussy with his free hand. He spread my pussy lips open with his fingers as he stood me back up with his hand on the front of my neck. Our faces were now touching, our bodies pressed up against each other. He turned my head so his mouth was against my ear.

"I want you to cum all over my dick as you watch these other people fucking in front of us. Enjoy all that you see as I enjoy this sweet pussy of mine. Take off your robe and shoes and then let me feel exactly how turned on you are." I obliged, realizing in that moment that Noah was about to make one of my wildest fantasies a reality. My heartbeat sped up and the shyness I felt when we first entered the room dissolved.

With his hand still around my neck, Noah shoved his hard dick all the way up inside my pussy. I screamed out in surprise and pleasure, which got the attention of a few couples around us. Still standing, I could see the realization of my biggest fantasy in front of us as people welcomed the newcomers with indulgent smiles.

As my shock wore off, Noah grabbed me by the hips and, without pulling out of me, lifted me onto the mattress as he climbed up behind me. Together we made our way further into the room. As I made myself comfortable in front of Noah, my ass high in the air with my chest on the bed, a beautiful blonde girl crawled over to us on her hands and knees and sat in front of us about six feet away.

She faced us, leaned back on her elbows, and spread her legs wide open in front of us. Her man, whose tattoos contrasted his white skin and glistened off his muscular build, wasn't far away, watching all the action, his dick sticking straight out in front of him. I noticed a few others also watching us as they continued in their personal playtime, their voyeurism on full display.

Propping herself up on one arm, Blondie played with herself, spreading her pussy wide open for Noah and me to watch. She had a beautiful pink pussy and small perfect tits that sat up on her thin frame. Noah pushed forward against me, moving us both closer before pushing my hips down toward the floor so that I was lying on my stomach. My hands were free to reach out and touch her. I preferred to watch, and as Noah repositioned himself on top of me, I folded my arms underneath my chin so that I could watch this chick play with herself as she watched Noah fuck me from the back.

I arched my back as hard as I could. Noah worked his way deep into my pussy as he hit it hard over and over. My pussy throbbed around his dick, indicating I was about to cum. He sped up his pace until my breath quickened and I let out a deep moan.

My noises clearly turned Blondie on and she began panting. Her legs shook as she let out cute little squeals before throwing her head back and letting out a cry of pleasure. Seeing a stranger cum on herself from watching me fuck sent me over the edge as I gushed hard all over Noah's dick.

As soon as Blondie finished cumming, her man lay her all the way down on her back, got on top of her and slid his dick deep inside her, slowly and deeply stroking her pussy as she caught her breath.

I reached my hand back and tapped Noah on the arm, signaling my desire to turn over. He lifted himself off me into a pushup position as I flipped over onto my back underneath him.

"You good, baby?" he asked, searching my face.

I smiled up at him. "That was so hot."

I closed my eyes and let out a deep breath. He kissed me softly on the mouth.

"Wanna check out another spot?"

I nodded and Noah held out his hand. He pulled me to an upright position and we both made our way toward the end of the mattress. I stepped off the mattress and then used Noah's shoulder to balance as I slipped my heels back on, one at a time. As I did so, I realized that Noah hadn't cum yet. He seemed unbothered, and it hit me how in hindsight, the amount of sex he had been initiating the past week seemed so intentional. It was all leading up to this night.

Noah

My goal was to make Blair cum to awaken the beast inside her. With a night like tonight, I knew she would never be satisfied with just one orgasm, and she'd be hungry and open for more. As soon as she came, I helped her to her feet and helped her with her shoes. I grabbed her by the hand and led her out of the room to the open couch area and we took a seat. Blair wanted to watch what was going on around us and scout out any potential for couples fun. We hadn't really seen anyone that either of us was attracted to, but we hadn't given up hope just yet.

The blonde girl with the pretty pussy and her man came out of the couples-only room and sat on the other side of Blair on the long couch we sat on. They began to chat it up while I scanned the room, looking for any opportunities. The more I looked around, the more I realized that if we wanted extra fun we might have to create it ourselves.

While Blair talked and laughed, I slid my hand up her thigh and opened her robe to play with her pussy. A few bystanders started looking on as the blonde girl played with her own pussy while I dug my fingers deep into Blair's. Just then, the coke-bottle Latina and her anaconda-dick boyfriend came out of one of the private rooms. We should have known it was her screams we heard when we came out of the locker rooms. Clearly they had moved on from the dance floor as well and decided to kick it up a notch.

Mr. Anaconda led his lady by the hand right toward us. He spun her around, pushed her forward so her chest was bent over the ottoman in front of us, positioned himself behind her and started fucking her doggy style just a few feet away. She let out a deep moan as he entered her raw and as he continued, we confirmed that it was indeed her screams we had heard coming out of the room before.

Blair looked over at me with a devilish grin, and as she watched this couple in front of us, I could feel her pussy getting wetter and wetter in my hand. After about a minute or two, Ms. Coke Bottle arched her back and pulled herself up onto her hands and looked directly at Blair. Her man slowed down his ruthless pounding just enough so this chick could catch her breath. She and Blair smiled at each other and with a wink, the girl opened her mouth to speak.

"I want to know if I have your permission to taste this delicious man you're with? Please, can I taste him?"

Shock colored Blair's face as she looked over at me. Ms. Coke Bottle maintained her position, her face just a foot or so away from ours.

I looked intently at Blair, letting her know the decision was entirely hers to make. I thought about the many possibilities that her answer may set forth and privately wished she would grant Ms. Coke Bottle the permission she sought. I badly craved to see how Blair would fare when up against the anaconda.

Blair looked deep into my eyes and I could tell her brain was running a mile a minute as she thought seriously before giving her answer. Suddenly, a grin danced across her lips and the right side of her mouth curled like it does when she gets caught doing something naughty.

She raised her eyebrows and without saying anything to me, looked back at Ms. Coke Bottle. "I would love to watch you taste all of him the way you did your man on the dance floor earlier."

I was taken aback, albeit impressed with her response. I did an internal victory dance and my dick grew harder picturing Blair being pounded by the anaconda. I couldn't get the thought out of my head.

With permission granted, Mr. Anaconda gripped Coke Bottle's hips and effortlessly lifted her torso while shifting his angle, placing her so that her face landed just inches away from my hard, upright dick. She steadied herself on the couch with one hand and grabbed the base of my dick with the other. She smiled over at Blair one last time, mouthed "thank you," spit on my dick, and swallowed the entire thing down her throat as her man picked back up his pace. Her mouth was warm and, due to how turned on I was by my thoughts of Blair, the occasional graze of her teeth didn't bother me in the least. I couldn't begrudge a little teeth action considering this chick was taking it from all angles.

Ms. Coke Bottle took my dick all the way down her throat every time, gagging on it and creating more spit. After no time at all, my dick slid effortlessly in and out of her mouth. I could feel her throat muscles contract and vibrate as she moaned from the massive dick going deep inside her pussy from the back.

She pulled my dick out of her mouth and with her hand still on the base, began to suck wildly on the head of my shaft as her cheeks formed a suction on my dick. She never let the tip out of her mouth entirely, creating dimples in her cheeks whenever she pulled away.

I still had my fingers inside Blair's pussy and I had never felt her wetter. She was clearly turned on by another female sucking my dick right in front of her and the thought alone made my dick pulsate inside Coke Bottle's mouth.

Coke Bottle must have thought I was about to cum as she took my entire dick deep into her throat one last time, sucking clean all the spit off me as she came up for air. Just then, she looked me dead in the eye and said, "I know her pussy is super wet, can I see for myself? She looks so yummy, I want to drink her."

I knew she was asking me as a courtesy, but again, the decision was not mine to make. I nodded toward Blair. "You'll have to ask her."

We both smiled and turned to look at Blair, who had a big grin on her face.

By this time, we had drawn quite the crowd around us. There was not a seat empty in the room, and a bunch of single girls, guys, and couples had gathered around to watch our sexy scene. Everyone, including myself, was awaiting Blair's response with bated breath. Blair looked directly into Coke Bottle's eyes and breathed, "Come taste this pussy, baby."

And with Blair's words, Mr. Anaconda lifted up Coke Bottle's torso again, shifting his angle as he took a step closer and placed Coke Bottle's face directly in front of Blair. Coke Bottle put each of her hands on top of Blair's thighs. She opened Blair's robe further and removed my hand from in between Blair's legs. Then one at a time, she put each arm around Blair's waist and nose-dived into Blair's pussy.

Blair leaned back and opened her legs to give Coke Bottle a better angle. Blair reached over and squeezed my arm, and I grabbed her hand to let her know I was right there with her. Her breathing deepened and she began to moan softly as Coke Bottle focused on Blair's clit. I could tell she was about to make Blair cum because all of a sudden Blair got real quiet.

She always held her breath before she came and I urged her, "Come on, baby, let it go ... cum for her, baby, let her have it."

Blair

With this chick eating the hell out of my pussy and Noah talking shit in my ear, I could barely hold my orgasm in much longer. My moans had attracted an impressive audience and it put even more pressure on me to give them the ending they had all been waiting for. It surprised me how willing my body was to cum so quickly, despite being surrounded by so many strangers. I sure loved to be watched, but I wasn't sure if my body would comply.

By this time, Coke Bottle had pulled away from Mr. Anaconda and was now on her knees in front of me. I held my breath and moved my hips up and down against her face as she stuck her tongue out hard against my clit.

I squeezed Noah's hand as hard as I could as he urged me to cum all over this chick's face. I looked at him right before I came and then closed my eyes tight and let out a cry of pleasure as my pussy pulsated and my juices leaked out all over Coke Bottle's face. I sat there catching my breath as Coke Bottle smiled hard at me and sat back on her feet as she licked her lips.

"Yummy!" she exclaimed as she used my knees to help push herself up to her feet.

She went over to Mr. Anaconda and stuck her tongue down his throat so that he could taste me, too, and then he whispered something in her ear. At the same time, Noah leaned over to me, kissed me softly behind my ear and whispered, "You are the sexiest woman alive. Now come with me, baby ..." He got to his feet.

Our audience had dissipated by this point but I covered myself with my robe shyly. He held out his hand for me to take and helped me up. Coke Bottle led Mr. Anaconda by the hand into one of the private rooms as Noah led me in the same direction. While Coke Bottle was eating my pussy, the guys must have planned to share a room together, since we walked right into the same room the two of them went into.

Noah closed the door behind him and we were face to face with these strangers. I got a good look at Mr. Anaconda for the first time. He was about six-foot-two, deep chocolate brown skin, a symmetrical face with a well-defined jawline and nice full lips. He had left his robe in the other room and was completely nude. He had a nice solid structure with great muscle composition, and then there was that tree trunk he was carrying around with him.

Up close, it was even bigger than it had looked as it disappeared over and over down this tiny girl's throat. I stared at it for a few seconds, and then couldn't help but to look over at his girl. None of it made sense, but my pussy began to throb again thinking about having the chance to find out for myself.

As I looked Coke Bottle up and down, she walked toward me. She had also left her robe in the other room, and now that I could see her standing up directly in front of me, the nickname Coke Bottle hardly did her figure justice. Her body was out of a magazine and all I could think about was watching her ride Noah's dick and seeing his hands gripping her every curve.

She reached both hands out and slid my robe off my shoulders, and we both let it fall to the floor. I still had on my Valentine's Day gift; well, half of it. I stepped out of my heels and stretched my feet. Mr. Anaconda lay back on the bed next to me as Coke Bottle then crossed to remove Noah's robe. She began kissing his chest while maintaining eye contact with me to gauge my reaction. I smiled back at her, letting her know that I didn't want her to stop and then I looked over at Mr. Anaconda. I became super shy and had no idea what my next move was supposed to be. Thankfully, Noah's voice broke the silence.

"That's all for you if you want it, baby. Do you? You want that dick, don't you, baby? You think you can take it?" he challenged me.

I looked at him as he spoke and then down at Coke Bottle. She had gotten down on her knees and had Noah's dick in her mouth again, her eyes on me. She slowly nodded with Noah's dick still in her mouth, egging me to answer his questions and giving me permission to say yes. And it was true. I desperately wanted to feel what that massive dick felt like inside my tight little pussy.

"I do, baby. I want to take it all. I CAN take it all and I will. Watch me!"

I looked over and down at Mr. Anaconda. He smiled at me and put his hand out. I laid my hand in his and he effortlessly pulled me on top of him. I steadied myself and grabbed the base of his thick shaft and felt that he had already slipped on a condom. On the floor next to the bed I could see the gold triple XL Magnum wrapper. I didn't even know they made condoms that big!

I put one hand on his chest and guided the tip of his rock-hard dick toward my pussy. It was so long I had to lean to one side just to fit it underneath me. I ran it up and down my clit, spreading my juices all over it. Once his dick was nice and wet, I slid it to the base of my pussy.

Slowly, I lowered my body onto his dick and could feel the walls of my pussy stretching to take his thickness. About halfway down, I came back up to allow my cum to build back up around the head of his shaft as I prepared to go all the way this time. I let out a deep moan as I slid myself all the way down on him. I closed my eyes to concentrate and when I felt my thighs spread out on top of him I opened them back up.

Anaconda was focused intently on my facial expressions, a smirk playing across his lips as he had likely seen similar expressions on every woman he'd ever slept with. He cocked his right eyebrow at me and nodded, impressed. With the sensation of his dick in my stomach, I looked over at

Noah, who was also admiring my expressions. He was lying on his back as well, Coke Bottle sitting up straight on top of him. Neither of them moved as they watched me take Anaconda's dick like a pro.

I lifted my chin in triumph. "See, baby, I told you I could take it all. Now show me how you fuck this bombshell sitting in your lap."

I slowly moved up and down on Mr. Anaconda, loosening up my tight pussy walls. It took about a minute or so of him being completely still; I kept reminding him to be gentle and let me create space for him to fuck me like I've been waiting for. He then slowly moved his hips up to meet mine, fucking my pussy ever so slightly as I took him in and out.

The harder he fucked me, the louder I got—the screaming we had heard before was not the least bit fake. I usually was more of a moaner, but with this massive dick I literally could not stop myself from screaming out in pleasure and pain. Every time this man went all the way deep inside me, I got a sensation in my stomach that I'd never experienced before. It didn't exactly hurt, but it was borderline uncomfortable.

At last, the pleasure of my pussy stretching out around his rock-hard dick overwhelmed me and I reached closer and closer to climax. Everyone else in the room had made me cum tonight, and now it was Anaconda's turn.

I reached out and grabbed his shoulder to let him know I wanted him to sit up. He obeyed, and with his dick still inside me, pulled himself up so that I could wrap my legs around him to sit in his lap. This was an entirely new sensation to get used to as his dick was angled more toward the back. I knew I would cum in this position and gyrated my hips against him, keeping his dick deep inside me. He then reached around and grabbed my ass with both hands, bouncing me up and down on his dick and hitting directly on my G-spot. At this point, my breath quickened and my pussy throbbed. It wouldn't be long until my release. I braced myself, knowing that while I was cumming I would, for the first time, be relinquishing all power to this stranger.

I held my breath and let Anaconda fuck me as hard as he could. I buried my head in his neck and let out a shriek of pleasure that surely the entire place could hear. My orgasm seemed to last forever as this man slowed his pace and moaned deeply into my chest. He hugged my body tightly against him and moved ever so slowly in and out of my soaking wet pussy. I could feel his dick throbbing even bigger inside me, opening up my pussy even more as he came inside me.

Noah

As soon as Blair challenged me to show her how I could fuck Coke Bottle, I got to work. Together, Coke Bottle and I had just witnessed Blair swallowing the biggest dick any of us had ever seen deep inside her pussy. It turned me on so much, and my dick was craving to feel the inside of Coke Bottle. Although I wasn't going to force it or even actively try to make it happen, I had wanted to fuck this chick since I saw her deep-throating her man on the dance floor. This opportunity just fell into our laps.

With Coke Bottle sitting on top of me, I reached down and guided my dick deep inside her pussy. I had grabbed a condom from the bowl of them next to the bed when we first walked in, and after Coke Bottle got my dick wet with her mouth, I slipped it on. I allowed Coke Bottle to ride my dick as I massaged her hips and thighs. She rode me like a rodeo bull rider as I raised my hips to meet her every time she slammed down on my dick.

I stared at Blair in the floor-to-ceiling mirrors, taking this massive dick all the way until it disappeared. I noticed Coke Bottle watching, too, so I sat up and flipped her onto her stomach. She lay flat, her face just feet away from the action, and I reached underneath her and pulled her hips up so her ass was wide open toward the sky. We both faced Blair and Anaconda and watched as the woman of mine arched her back and found her rhythm. Her legs were spread as open as she could handle as Anaconda pounded her from underneath.

I looked down to watch my own dick disappearing all the way inside Coke Bottle's pussy as she creamed all over my dick. I pulled all the way out of her, bent down to spit on her pussy and rammed my dick all the way inside her, causing her to scream out. I pushed deep inside her, then pulled all the way out of her repeatedly, making her squirt all over me.

I was so hard that I could steady my hips and hit my target every time while I watched Blair, her legs now wrapped around this guy, making Anaconda's massive dick disappear over and over. Blair worked her hips around in a circle and I could tell she was about to cum. The closer I could see Blair getting, the closer I got, until I heard her scream out. I lost all control as I fucked Coke Bottle with all my might, closing my eyes and imagining it being Blair in front of me as I busted all inside Coke Bottle.

Blair damn near collapsed on the bed next to Mr. Anaconda as she caught her breath. I pulled out of Coke Bottle and reached over to the table in the corner and threw everyone a towel to clean themselves off. Everyone was glowing, but it was clear that Anaconda wanted to go for a second round with Blair. Despite being the ringleader for the whole night, Coke Bottle made it clear that her man was not available for seconds. She went over to him and sat on his lap, still smiling. He put his arm around her and rested his hand on her bare thigh, almost reluctantly. Blair, always conscious of her surroundings, got off the bed and stood right in front of them. She took Coke Bottle's face in her hands and kissed her softly on the mouth.

With the girl's face still in her hands, Blair whispered, "Thank you for everything tonight. You guys are wonderful. I hope your Valentine's Day was as lovely as ours has been."

Blair kissed her again, winked at Mr. Anaconda and skipped over to me, grabbing me by the hand and pulling me out of the room. We left Ms. Coke Bottle and Mr. Anaconda in our love nest, never to be seen or heard from again.

Once outside the room, Blair turned and smiled at me. "Well that was something," she said conclusively.

I laughed. "Yeah, I don't think it gets better than that! Let's grab that bottle and we'll have a nightcap at home. What do you say?"

"Sounds good to me. I don't think I can handle any more tonight. As great as Anaconda felt, I do not at all envy Coke Bottle. That's a lot to handle on a daily basis." She shook her head back and forth in disbelief.

"You have no idea. I'm proud to say I'm happy with what I've been blessed with. It was so hot to see you take the whole thing, though." I reached around Blair to grab her ass and pulled her into me.

"I'm happy with what you were blessed with, as well." Blair smiled at me before nibbling on my bottom lip.

I kissed her passionately. "Let's go home, baby. I need to be inside you one last time tonight."

Showtime

Adam

My fiancée, Nicole, had just received a huge bonus at work. I decided to surprise her with a celebration weekend getaway that included VIP tickets to her favorite artist's stadium tour concert in Los Angeles. An old college buddy of mine happened to be part owner of the Rose Bowl and was able to hook us up with three tickets—one each for Nicole and I, and one for my dear friend Angie, our hostess for the weekend. Angie had a huge loft apartment just minutes away from the stadium with a spare bedroom that she was more than thrilled to provide us.

We hopped on the next thing smokin' to L.A. The heat and humidity hit us like a smack in the face as soon as we left the airport. We were grateful to have some spare time to cool down and get nice and settled in at Angie's place before heading to the concert.

Nicole and Angie had never met before, but they hit it off right away, dancing and singing along with every word. Nicole was on such a high after her bonus and the opportunity to see her favorite show that she was attracting energy from all angles. She made friends with everyone around us as I watched, enjoying *The Nicole Show* even more than the amazing concert. I loved to see her in all her power, confidently creating the exact atmosphere around her to feed her insatiable lust for life.

Our VIP tickets included access to the official after-party at a club downtown, where there was sure to be many celebrities and even more great energy for Nicole to utilize to her advantage. It was bound to be a night for the books.

The three of us decided to head back to the apartment to freshen up before heading to the party. Once we got back to the loft, I was so worked up from all the energy at the concert that I had to get my hands on Nicole. After watching her star in her own show, I simply couldn't wait until after the party and so I joined her in the shower she had started for herself.

Nicole

After all the dancing and drinking and singing, I was on a high like never before. Never had I ever been front row at a concert, and to witness my favorite artist up close made me feel like I had just been on a fucking spree for days. I reluctantly left Adam to hop my sweaty ass in the shower before heading to the after-party.

I was deliciously surprised when he snuck his way in to join me just minutes later. As if I needed any more stimulation to heighten my energy—the thought of fucking in someone else's shower while she was in the next room got my pussy throbbing.

I had my eyes closed, facing the hot water as it streamed down my face and onto my plump breasts when I felt Adam's hands reach underneath my arms. He squeezed both nipples between his fingers, which sent a shiver throughout my body. The contrast of the hot water and the goosebumps from Adam's touch was most intense deep inside my pussy. I felt it growing wetter and wetter. Without saying a word, he wasted no time, knowing we only had a little while before Angie would come knocking, telling us to hurry up so we could get to the party already. I could feel his massive hard-on poking at my ass as he massaged and lifted my breasts up while biting and sucking on my neck. I reached behind me and spread my ass cheeks apart and he slid his dick all the way up inside me without saying a word.

I reached for the handle that was on the wall of the shower for support as he pounded away at my pussy. He grabbed my leg and propped my foot on the side of the tub so that he could get deeper. I could feel his dick in my stomach. With his hand now on the middle of my back, he pushed my torso forward.

"Grab that towel, baby, and bite down hard on it so that Angie doesn't hear what I'm about to do to you," he demanded.

He stopped moving behind me momentarily as I reached out of the shower and grabbed the hand towel hanging on the wall, shoving a bunch of it in my mouth as I prepared myself as best I could for whatever Adam had in store for me. After completely owning my power at the concert, it was so sexy to have this man bossing me around, and I gladly complied with his every command. My pussy pulsated at the very thought of allowing him to take me any way he wanted. I was entirely his.

Adam was fidgeting with something behind me as he pulled his dick out of my pussy. Not knowing what was next, I braced myself and waited, my breath quickening in anticipation. I then felt a cool sensation at the opening of my pussy and the pressure of something being pushed inside me. Adam successfully worked the entire shampoo bottle in and began to fuck me with it as I moaned in pleasure. It was so wide and the consistent girth of the plastic made my pussy walls stretch to accommodate it.

With the bottle inside me and my pussy walls hugging it tightly, Adam reached his hand around in front of me and played with my clit. With his other hand, he placed his dick on my ass and gently pushed it inside me. He made sure his body was close enough to mine to keep the bottle in place as his big dick in my ass fought for room. My eyes rolled back in my head and I was grateful for the towel in my mouth. I bit down hard on it as the pain of having all my holes filled transformed into amazing pleasure.

Adam

I knew that I wasn't going to be able to last long after all the stimulation from the concert, and I badly wanted to cum inside of Nicole to mark my territory for the night before she was off and running again, gathering up all the energy she could at the after-party. With the shampoo bottle all the way inside Nicole's tight pussy, my dick was even snugger in her ass than usual. The increased tightness had me feeling like I could cum after only a few pumps, and I knew it was only a matter of time before Angie started to bug us, as well. Just then, Nicole moved my hand off her clit and began to play with herself as she held on for dear life with her other hand. She began to moan uncontrollably, the towel gag still in her mouth as she came, pushing the shampoo bottle out of her pussy as she squirted with such force. I grabbed both her hips, no longer worried about keeping the bottle in place and pounded her ass three times as hard as I could before I felt myself cumming.

"Oh fuck, baby," I moaned deeply as I shot my load deep in her ass.

Just as I slowed my pace, emptying myself entirely inside her, she let the towel in her mouth fall to the floor of the shower as she gasped for breath, inhaling deeply before letting out a long moan. As I pulled out of her slowly, she stood up and tilted her head backward and rested it on my shoulder.

"Hi, baby," she said with a smile, her eyes closed. I kissed her softly on the cheek as the water ran down both our bodies.

"Hi to you, baby." I gently spun her around to face me. "Sorry about the shower attack. Watching you all night … mmm …" I trailed off. "I couldn't wait until after the party to have you."

She stood on her tippy toes and kissed me deeply on the mouth. "I wouldn't have had it any other way, my love." She reached for the washcloth. "But now you owe me a rubdown," she teased.

We took turns cleaning each other before Angie called to us from the other room.

"We'll be right there, we're just getting dressed," I yelled back, the white lie easing Angie off our backs for a little. We turned off the water and I handed Nicole a towel for her to dry off.

She blew out her hair as I got dressed and then she slid into a dress that she had been waiting for the right occasion to wear. It was a red, short-sleeve, body-hugging mini dress. It drove me wild the moment I saw how it accentuated her every curve. I went out to the living room to check on Angie while Nicole did her makeup.

"Finally," Angie said as she rolled her eyes at the sight of me. "Thought you guys might have fallen asleep; you were being too quiet there for awhile."

"Oh, thank God," I thought to myself with a smile. "She didn't hear the near rape in her shower that just took place."

Angie was raring to go, with a drink poured and waiting for us to enjoy before we left for the party. Nicole came out shortly after and we all made a toast.

"To an unforgettable night with unforgettable friends," I said, short and sweet.

We headed across town to the after-party, at a club called Playhouse that none of us had ever been to. We hadn't been in the party for more than a few minutes when I ran into an old college friend, Tanya. She was model height in heels, slender framed, with a sexy ass short bob haircut, and still with all the curves in the right places that I remembered from college. I felt the blood rushing to my dick the moment I realized it was her. We walked toward her and she lit up as soon as she recognized me, giving me a big hug. I introduced her to Nicole, to whom she gave an even bigger hug.

It had been nearly ten years since I had seen her and she was still drop-dead gorgeous, even more so after finding out it was two kids that helped her figure become a bit more curvy. She was recently divorced and in L.A. for business. Knowing some local record producers, she had found herself at this after-party.

Nicole was more than happy for us to be catching up and dominating the conversation, as she could not stop looking at this Amazon in front of us. After a minute or two, I noticed that Tanya looked as though she was needing to finish up the conversation we had interrupted, and so when Nicole offered to get us all a drink, I decided to go with her.

We excused ourselves, telling Tanya we would be right back. Once at the bar and out of earshot of Tanya, Nicole couldn't stop raving to me how gorgeous she thought Tanya was.

"Who the hell is this Tanya chick and why haven't you ever mentioned her before?" Nicole asked. "She's gorgeous, baby," she added.

All I could do was smile and nod. I explained that I had a thing for her back in college, but that she would never give me the time of day.

"This one time I got stuck at her apartment during a snowstorm and couldn't get back to campus so I crashed at her place, and of course I tried to make a move on her. I got her tipsy and she let me take her shirt off, but she always thought I was too much of a ladies' man and didn't want to get involved," I explained, honestly.

"I think she always had a thing for me but it didn't go anywhere. Knowing me, I would have smashed and passed anyways ..." I trailed off, my dick growing again at the thought of those perky tits in my face nearly a decade ago. I snapped back to reality.

"You like her, huh, baby?" I asked, and Nicole blushed slightly. She had a hungry look in her eye as she stared at Tanya, and I could tell Nicole had just zeroed in on her energy source for the night.

"She's all yours if you want her," I encouraged her.

Nicole

Adam kept the drinks flowing heavy and seemed to be enjoying the fact that Tanya and I were hitting it off nicely. I was grateful that Adam had originally followed me to the bar to give me the 411 on Tanya. We had a relationship rule to always divulge even the smallest details about someone from our past in order for the other person to be able to move in strength and truth so that neither of us got sideswiped later by finding out something that made them look foolish in front of others. It helped us to stay connected even when we weren't physically next to each other. Knowing the facts was nothing, however, compared to the thought of those tits of hers all in my man's face, coupled with the fact that she hadn't given him any play, and I was smitten. It became my mission to see what, if anything, she'd be willing to give up tonight.

I looked around and noticed that Angie was dirty dancing with the kind of guy she said was "her type": tall, chocolate, handsome, and barely legal. I knew that she would be kept occupied for a while, and so I decided to get comfy with Tanya. We danced for a while, working up a sweat as we laughed and chatted. Adam watched us intently, likely pondering how he had gotten so lucky to witness his lust-filled college crush and the love of his life all over each other on the dance floor. Every so often, he'd come over to replace our drinks, making sure we were good.

"Great, baby. Thank you!" I yelled over the music. He retreated to his spot at the bar, not wanting to disrupt the energy Tanya and I were creating between us.

The more we danced, the more consumed I became with how I was going to take things to the next level without coming on too strong. Although we were dancing and touching, I couldn't really tell if Tanya was attracted to me sexually. The fine line between innocent flirting and actual desire was always so exhilarating to explore. The more I thought about it, the more I craved her body all over mine.

"Does she know that as she grinds her ass back on me she's hitting my clit every time?" I mused. "Does she know just how wet my pussy is at the mere thought of how badly I want to taste her juices?"

The desire for this woman was more than I could handle on my own; I'd need to enlist Adam to help me. He was always the person I went to when I needed help achieving something, so I figured Tanya would be no exception. He looked at her like she was his next meal, and I knew that he would be more than willing to allow me to utilize him in any way necessary for me to conquer my desires that evening. After all, what better way for me to get closer to Tanya than for a mutual interest to bridge the gap? I had a strong feeling that giving them what I knew they both wanted would inspire them to return the favor and give me what I wanted, as well.

I finally mustered up the courage and whispered in Tanya's ear. "I know it's been a long time since you and Adam have seen each other ... I think you should take him upstairs and give him one of those old college tongue kisses I've heard so much about."

She pulled away from me slightly with a shocked look on her face. It was clear that she never in her wildest dreams expected me to share him that night, and as her look of shock turned into a devilish grin, I could tell that she was into it.

"Seriously?" she asked, apprehensively. It was so sexy to see her respond with such intrigue; she clearly had no idea what kind of woman she was dealing with.

"Seriously," I repeated. "This night is about everyone enjoying themselves, and I know how much Adam would like to have another go at you. Please," I urged. "For me."

She grabbed my face with both her hands and kissed me passionately on the mouth.

"Jeez!" I thought. My plan was working already!

"You have my full permission to settle any unfinished business," I said.

The smile vanished from Tanya's face, replaced by determination.

The confidence I had in myself and my man was clearly something Tanya had never experienced, and her change in attitude seemed to suggest that she wanted to make me proud. As I watched Tanya strut over to where Adam stood at the bar, my pussy began to pulsate with the thought of getting the chance to have more of this beautiful woman.

Adam

As I was watching the two of them playfully lighting up the room on the dance floor, I saw Nicole whisper something in Tanya's ear that inspired her to grab Nicole by the face and kiss her on the mouth. I could tell by the look on Nicole's face that she was just as surprised as I was, but she definitely welcomed it. I was no stranger to the impact Nicole's energy and aura had on people everywhere she went, but to see Tanya, the gorgeous but straight-edged girl I knew back in college, kiss her on the mouth in front of everyone was unexpected to say the least.

Even more unexpected was that directly after she kissed Nicole, Tanya set her sights on me, and before I knew it, she was standing right in front of me.

I looked over at Nicole, who was still standing where Tanya had left her on the dance floor. She smiled at me and nodded suggestively but intently, as if to say, "Follow her lead, baby." I looked back at Tanya, who was now inches away from my face.

She leaned in to me. "I have something I want to tell you, but I can barely hear myself think over this music. Follow me upstairs," she commanded, and then grabbed my arm and spun me around, leading me to the stairs.

I looked back at Nicole to gauge her reaction. She smiled her evil, sexy smile at me. I gave her my best, "What the fuck?" look and she laughed and shrugged, pretending not to know what was happening.

"Go," she mouthed insistently as she waved her hand, shooing me away. It was all the permission I needed.

"What in the hell do these two have up their sleeves?" I thought.

As I followed Tanya, she took her time placing her long legs on each ascending stair. She didn't pull her dress down when it naturally rode up from the upward movements of her legs, making sure that I could see her black G-string under her little black dress. Then, just as she was nearing the top step, she bent over as if to fix the strap on her stiletto, giving me a front-row seat to the show in between her legs. After all these years, I had the view that I always wanted back in college: Tanya's ass in my face and those sweet pussy lips staring straight at me.

I wasn't worried about getting caught looking, as Nicole encouraged me to let Tanya take me upstairs, but I had to wonder why my girl would send me away from everyone with another woman. And not just any woman, the one who was dancing and grinding on her just moments before, and whose tits had been in my face once upon a time ago. I put those curiosities to the back of my mind for now to focus on what Tanya had to tell me.

Once we got all the way upstairs, we entered a bar, where I ordered us a round of drinks to keep things escalating. The bartender placed both drinks in front of us and Tanya grabbed hers to take a sip.

"What is it that you wanted to—" I said before Tanya pressed one finger against my mouth and cut me off.

She removed her finger and I decided it was best to let her do the talking. I reached for my drink. Just as my fingertips grazed the condensation on the cold glass, Tanya grabbed my hand and brought it to her mouth, sucking on my fingers before sliding my hand between her legs. She was so wet she had soaked through her panties, and I wondered if it had been Nicole's energy or mine that had created the slip and slide that was Tanya's pussy.

"Nicole!" I thought to myself. With my hand between another woman's legs, all I could think about was the devilish grin Nicole gave me and the hand gesture she made urging me to follow Tanya away from her.

"Relax," Tanya purred in my ear, "she sent me here." She grabbed my wrist and pulled my hand farther between her legs.

I had no idea what that meant, but I decided to go with it. Tanya's soaking wet panties slipped easily to the side and I slid two fingers inside her warm pussy. I was immediately brought back to that snowy night in college. My dick grew harder and harder in my pants as I massaged Tanya's G-spot and finger fucked her for the first time. My thoughts then wandered back to Nicole, whom I decided was definitely the reason this woman's pussy was soaking wet to the core. Suddenly, the realization hit me like a rock: Nicole was using me to pull Tanya in so I could help Nicole finish what she had started on the dance floor.

"That sly bitch of mine!" I thought to myself, fully embracing the mission I was now a part of.

I had quickened the pace of my fingers sliding in and out of this chick's pussy, when she suddenly pulled my hand away and seductively sucked her pussy juices off my fingers.

I shook my head. I had no idea what Nicole's plans were for Tanya, but I trusted she would reveal them sooner rather than later. I once again pushed all those thoughts aside, focusing on the task in front of me.

Tanya finished licking herself off my fingers and moved even closer to me, moving her face next to my ear to tell me what she brought me upstairs for.

"Adam, I've always wanted to feel your fingers inside me …" She brushed my ear with her breath. "That look on your face when you first touched my pussy was so worth waiting all these years for. But I want to feel your hard dick inside me too, Adam." She moaned and kissed my ear. "I know I didn't give you a chance back in college, but I want you now. I want to see what you taste like down my throat. I want to see how wet you can get this pussy."

She then grabbed the hot sauce out of the caddy on the bar and I watched her unscrew the top. She completely covered the tip of her finger and as I looked down to watch a few drops hit the floor, my dick was bulging visibly through my pants.

"Yeah … you and me both, buddy," I thought silently.

I looked back at her hand and watched her touch herself with the finger she had poured hot sauce all over. With her hand still between her legs, she leaned in toward me again and in my ear whispered, "My pussy is now on fire and tingling for you, Adam. Come cool it off for me," she pleaded, begging me to drop to my knees and eat her pussy in front of everyone right there.

Although there was only a handful of people in the room, no way in hell was I going to put my face anywhere near this woman's pussy without Nicole around. She would likely be more pissed at me that she didn't get to witness it, if anything, but it was not something I was willing to risk. And as if she could read my mind, I looked up and saw Nicole standing by the stairs, watching both of us with a grin on her face.

Nicole

I figured I had given Tanya enough time alone with Adam to get them both fired up for what I planned to do next. What I was witnessing was so intense between them, but I could tell Adam was uncomfortable with Tanya's aggressiveness. We had never discussed what we were comfortable with in a situation like this. He saw me out of the corner of his eye and stared at me, pleading with his gaze for me to direct his next move. I simply stood there, too turned on to interrupt, and nodded with a smile, letting Adam know he was exactly where I wanted him.

I was completely consumed by their passion, perhaps even more so than they were. It was so sexy to see Adam totally mesmerized as an outsider. It was one thing to feel Adam's burning intensity for me, and I knew he was utterly smitten with me, but to witness his raw energy for another woman who I was also totally enamored with was out of this world hot.

Adam's focus turned back to Tanya as he took his fingers to his mouth, gathering spit on them before putting them back between her legs. This time, he aggressively shoved his fingers up inside her pussy so much that she stood on her tippy toes to take his long fingers deep inside her. I figured he was making sure to spread the hot sauce as deep inside her as he could so that her pussy tingled for him from the inside out. My pussy walls trembled at the thought of how on fire her pussy must be and how pleasurable his fingers must feel at the same time. I crossed the bar to them before my brain even had the chance to register my movement.

I gently put my hand on Adam's arm, letting him know I was standing right next to him, and removed his hand from between Tanya's legs. His fingers were dripping and completely saturated with her juices. I looked Tanya directly in the eyes as I sucked her pussy off of Adam's fingers. I could taste her sweet nectar against the spicy hot sauce and the combination was too delicious not to share. I didn't swallow, instead took Tanya's face in my hands and kissed her deeply, pushing her tasty flavors into her mouth with my tongue. We shared the flavor between us until we couldn't taste it any longer and all that was left was the tingling of our tongues dancing around each other's.

I pulled away and in Tanya's ear I whispered, "I have to taste that for real ... come with me."

I grabbed her hand and led her to the darkened, empty VIP section that was across from the bar. That night, everyone was VIP, and so the club had no use for the space.

I thought to myself, "I'll put this space to good use, no problem!"

Adam followed closely behind us and I directed him to sit down on one of the couches along the wall. I then sat Tanya down on the ottoman facing Adam and walked around behind her.

As I bent over and kissed her neck, she leaned her head backward against my shoulder. I reached around the front of her and spread her legs wide open, giving Adam a full frontal view of her deliciously wet pussy. Her panties were still pulled to the side, which pushed her pussy lips together, making them look extra juicy right in front of his face. I rubbed up and down on her smooth legs, now kneeling down behind her, both of us facing Adam.

I managed to catch Adam's eyes with mine, and as he stared back at me, I rubbed my fingers along Tanya's pussy lips and spread them wide open. Adam looked down at what I was doing to Tanya. I could see the big dick print in his pants and a yearning came from deep within my pussy walls to ride his dick while Tanya watched what it was like to take him all the way inside me, something I knew she wanted for herself. But first, I needed to taste the full effect of Tanya's little hot sauce trick.

I slowly walked around to face Tanya, and doing a quick check to make sure no one was around or watching us, I lifted my dress to expose my ass in Adam's face before I got down on my knees in front of Tanya. I could hear Adam gasp at both his realization that I had neglected to put on any panties, and at my completely unexpected move to taste Tanya right here in the club. I stared directly into Tanya's eyes as I ran my hands up both her thighs and onto her hips. I hooked both of my thumbs underneath the straps of her G-string and slowly pulled them down. She picked up each foot as she stepped out of her panties. I reached back and handed them to Adam.

"Keep these safe," I commanded.

He put them in his jacket pocket.

I wasted no time, wanting the sweet and spicy flavor that flowed out of Tanya in my mouth as soon as possible. I dove right into Tanya's pussy and my lips immediately burned from the hot sauce. She moaned in pleasure, and likely relief, that finally someone had come to extinguish the heat. It was a strange sensation to feel my lips numb up as my tongue went to town on her clit. She arched her back and let her head fall off the other side of the ottoman, giving me full access to her pussy.

As I swirled my tongue around and around on her clit, her legs lifted around my head; Adam had grabbed her ankles and placed each of her feet on his knees. He spread his legs apart, which in turn spread hers wide open to assist in my full-on attack. I drove my tongue inside her pussy, feeling another wave of heat from the hot sauce that Adam dug deep inside her.

The hot sauce mixed with her sweetness was such a unique flavor and I just couldn't get enough of it. I had plenty of experience with the taste of my own juices, habitually sucking on my fingers after playing with myself and often licking myself off of Adam after he pulled out of me, but my own brand didn't even touch how amazing Tanya tasted in my mouth. I had to remember this trick of hers for Adam to enjoy with me!

With her legs wide open and my face nose-deep inside her, her body shook, getting close to climax. I wanted to feel what it was like to be inside of her as she came, so I gently slid my fingers inside as I focused my tongue on her clit. She moaned softly as I found her G-spot, sending her over the edge. She threw her hand up to cover her mouth as she panted and moaned, her pussy gripping and strangling my fingers. I had never experienced the feeling, but it was enough to make my pussy gush at the thought of what it would feel like for Adam's big dick to be inside her. In that moment, I thanked the condom gods for reminding me to slip a few in my purse before we left Angie's place.

Adam

I was completely amazed at the eagerness Nicole had in wanting to taste Tanya in the middle of the club. It was like witnessing a baby after birth, searching relentlessly for the first suckle on her mother's breast. Nicole wanted Tanya badly, and was clearly willing to do just about anything to have her. As eager as she was, I wanted to make it as accessible to her as possible, so I grabbed Tanya's ankles and put them in my lap. I rubbed my hands up and down her smooth legs as Nicole's tongue ravaged between them with her ass bent over in my face. It was the most beautiful sight I had ever laid my eyes on, my rock-hard dick the true testament.

As soon as Nicole swallowed all of Tanya's cum, she sat up and placed each of Tanya's legs back on the floor. Tanya sat up and slid her dress back underneath her, but she kept her legs apart so I could see her swollen clit still throbbing.

Nicole stood up and turned around to face me. Seductively yet sternly she said to me "Now Adam, I want you to take your dick out so I can show Tanya how I ride it."

I was a bit shocked at her brazenness, but I had to admit it turned me on to see my girl in such command of the situation. She was going to dictate to both of us exactly how it would go down so she could also enjoy what Tanya and I had been waiting a decade for. She might have been the new kid on the block, but she was not going to let that stop her from being the ringleader.

I looked around, and still no one was around to pay us any mind. I had a feeling that even if I told Nicole no, she wouldn't have stopped until she got exactly what she wanted. Without saying a word, with Nicole standing expectantly in front of me, I unzipped my pants and did as I was told. Tanya gasped slightly when she saw my dick for the first time, not realizing that all these years, this was exactly what she missed out on in college.

Nicole turned around to face Tanya and moved my legs close together so she could straddle them. She reached behind her, and bending over with her ass in my face so she could see between her legs, grabbed the base of my dick. She squatted down slightly and rubbed the head of my dick around the inner lips of her pussy, making sure to get it nice and wet before she lowered herself inch by inch onto my dick for Tanya to watch.

Nicole

I lowered myself onto Adam's big, hard dick, maintaining eye contact with Tanya the whole time, her face three or so feet from the action. She had been surprised when she first saw what he was packing, and now she showed even more surprise at my expert ability to take it all with minimal effort.

"This is what years of practice looks like, honey," I thought to myself.

As I found my groove, I still didn't have an exact plan of how I was going to get Tanya to myself so that I could finally feel her tongue on my pussy. I knew that once she had gotten a piece of Adam, my chances would greatly decrease. No, Adam was going to have to be Tanya's standing ovation, not her opening act. I put those thoughts aside and figured with a little shit talking, I might inspire an idea.

"You like the size of his dick, don't you?" I asked Tanya.

"Very impressive," she breathed, not being able to take her eyes off his dick going in and out of my pussy.

"You like the way it looks disappearing all the way inside me, don't you?" I suggested.

"I do ..." she trailed off as she rubbed up and down her inner thighs with long, graceful fingers.

"You want to feel what this dick feels like inside you, don't you?"

She played with herself. "I do ..." she whispered.

"I want to hear you say it."

She looked me dead in the eyes, smiled, and said, "I want to feel exactly how he makes you feel."

I shook my head slowly back and forth, smiled at her and leaned in to kiss her on the mouth. I pulled away slightly so that our faces were an inch apart.

I waited a few moments before repeating, "I want to hear you say it."

With our faces almost touching, her eyes searched mine. She looked hungry, desperate, but cautious.

Then, in a quiet voice, she said, "I want to feel what that dick feels like inside me."

And with that admission, I sat back and came all over Adam's dick, holding my breath and clenching all my muscles to not make noise that could be heard over the music in the club. It was one of the hardest orgasms I had ever experienced. I was so turned on by this gorgeous woman in front of me admitting she wanted to fuck my man while playing with her sweet pussy. Adam grabbed my hips to hold me steady as I gushed all over him. Tanya rubbed her clit faster, every so often fucking herself with her fingers. I wanted her to cum again to make sure she flushed out all the hot sauce before Adam fucked her. As soon as I finished cumming, I focused my attention back on Tanya.

"You want to feel what you missed out on in college, don't you?" I continued, grinding slowly on Adam's dick.

"Oh yes," she breathed, her breaths quickening. "I want to feel exactly what I missed."

"And you want him to punish that pussy for ever telling him no, don't you?" I asked.

She was getting close to cumming now. "I want him to beat this bad pussy up," she moaned.

"And you want to taste his cum down your throat when he's finished, don't you?" Her body convulsed as she began to cum.

"I want to taste it nowwww!" she screamed as she came all over the ottoman she was laying on. I watched her juices leak out of her pussy and all over her fingers.

As Tanya came in front of us, I moved slightly to the side so that Adam could also see what I had just done to Tanya with my words. Her body was jerking and her head thrown back as she stuck her fingers deep inside herself. Just then, without saying a word, Adam grabbed me around the waist and lifted his hips, driving his dick hard and deep inside me repeatedly. I could feel he was about to cum. I squeezed my pussy as tight as I could around his dick, milking the orgasm right out of him.

"Feed her my cum, baby," he said hurriedly. His breath quickened and then stopped as he released himself deep into my pussy.

Although I was on birth control, it wasn't often that Adam came inside me, but this time was different. This time we were on a mission together and I immediately realized the missing piece in the Tanya puzzle. One of the things she most wanted all along was now inside my pussy, with only one way to get it. I kept my muscles squeezed tightly as I lifted myself up and off of Adam, making sure to keep all his cum inside me. I stood up and pulled my dress down as if nothing had happened and held my hand out to Tanya. She allowed me to help her off the couch and I pulled her in close to me.

"Follow me," I whispered in her ear as I led her toward the back where I could see a restroom sign in the distance.

"Fifteen minutes," I mouthed to Adam over my shoulder as we walked away.

The best part of these high-profile celebrity parties was that nothing was off limits when money was involved. I eagerly approached the bouncer that stood outside of the bathroom doors and noticed his name was Tony from his nametag.

"Hi, Tony," I moaned softly in his ear. "Keep an eye out for us, will ya? My girlfriend and I have some important business to take care of. My man will be right behind us, direct him where to go, please?" I asked sweetly. Adam would know to throw him a few dollars—this wasn't our first time getting busy in a bathroom.

He nodded and in his deep voice responded, "You got it, little lady." Tanya and I hurried past Tony and into the handicapped stall on the left.

Adam

Watching Tanya cum in front of Nicole and I after hearing her admit that she wanted to taste my cum "right now" brought me back to our original conversation by the bar when she admitted she wanted to find out what I tasted like. I knew that would be enough to get Tanya to go all the way with Nicole.

I pulled myself together and went to the balcony that overlooked the ground level dance floor. Angie, to no surprise, was still all over her tall, dark youngster, so I went back to the bar. I ordered myself a bottle of water and then looked down at my watch. It was almost time for me to meet the girls in the bathroom. I ordered us all another round, as I figured it would be appreciated after all the action, and headed toward the back.

The bouncer eyed me quizzically, as if expecting me. "What did these chicks say to him?" I wondered to myself.

"Last door on the left, sir," the bouncer said in his rich, bass voice, interrupting my thoughts. I thanked him and slipped a few bills into his hand and headed in.

I gently knocked on the door before opening it to find Nicole sitting back on the closed toilet seat, her ass hanging off the bottom with one leg propped up on the hand towel rack, the other wrapped around the back of Tanya's neck as Tanya licked and sucked on her pussy like a dog who hadn't had a sip of water in days.

I watched as Nicole squeezed my cum out of her pussy and into Tanya's mouth and fed it to her like feeding a baby bird. Tanya was on her knees in front of Nicole, her arms wrapped around on top of Nicole's thighs, pulling Nicole's pussy into her face as she sucked out every drop. It was the hottest thing to see these two chicks, dressed so pretty, doing something so dirty.

It was hard to tell whose moans were whose until Nicole looked up and saw me standing there. The moment she saw me, her moans took over as she began to cum all over Tanya's face. Tanya pulled her closer, not letting up her relentless tongue action on Nicole's clit. It felt like all the blood in my body rushed to my dick as I watched this scene in front of me: the love of my life with her long legs spread wide-the-fuck open directly in front of my dirtiest college fantasy licking and tongue-fucking an orgasm out of her.

I placed the drinks on the counter of the sink and out of the way. I unzipped my pants and let them fall to my ankles as I began to stroke my hard dick. I grabbed Nicole's purse to take out a condom and set it on the counter until further notice.

Tanya was still on her knees in front of Nicole as she kissed her clit softly, allowing Nicole to catch her breath. Nicole reached her arms out to Tanya and pulled her face to hers. She stuck her tongue in Tanya's mouth and they shared my cum between them. Nicole moaned audibly, and they both swallowed.

Nicole then pulled away and looked directly at Tanya. "It's your turn to feel what that big, hard dick feels like inside of you." Nicole looked up at me, directing Tanya to my presence.

Tanya turned around and the look of surprise on her face let me know that she hadn't known I was standing there. She stood up and took a step toward me, smiling at me sweetly. I took her by the chin and stuck my tongue into her mouth, tasting Nicole on her lips. She returned the kiss with hungry passion and I lifted her off her feet and wrapped her arms and legs around me. After all the fantasies, and that one lust-filled snowy night ... after a decade, and with the help of the woman I was going to make my wife, Tanya and I were finally going to have our chance to satisfy all cravings.

I could hear Nicole slide the waiting condom off the counter and rip open the package with her mouth. As I kissed Tanya, Nicole grabbed the base of my dick and slid it on. She then spat on my dick before sliding the whole thing down her throat, making it nice and wet before guiding it directly into Tanya's aching pussy.

Tanya and I both moaned as she took my whole dick all the way inside her. She was even wetter now than she had been at the top of the stairs, and my dick slid effortlessly in and out of her as I repeatedly lifted her ass up and slammed it down on my shaft. Her pussy felt different than Nicole's, but just as tight, and she moaned deeply in my ear with every thrust.

Nicole demanded, "Sit her down on the sink, baby, and punish that pussy for ever saying no to you."

I turned us around and did as I was told, gently lowering Tanya onto the counter. She kept her arms wrapped around the back of my neck as I put a pounding on that pussy.

"Give it to her harder. Nobody tells my baby no!" Nicole added, and I picked up my pace. Tanya's pussy walls began to throb around my dick and I could tell that she was getting off on the shit talking, so I decided to join in.

"You like hearing Nicole talk shit to you, huh?" I asked as I fucked her harder with every word.

"I fucking love it," she responded.

"And you loved eating both of our cum out of her pussy, didn't you?"

"I loved it," she breathed, hardly able to form full sentences.

"You never thought I'd let you have this dick, did you Tanya?" Nicole chimed back in.

"Never ..." she moaned into me as she bit my skin lightly, her mouth wide open against my shoulder.

"Thank you ... thank you ... thank you," she moaned repeatedly with every hard thrust I gave her.

"This pussy is ours now, you hear me?" I told Tanya, and I could feel her walls sweat harder and harder until she burst.

"It's all yours!" she screamed as her whole body convulsed underneath me. I fought to keep my dick inside her as her pussy tightened around me, nearly pushing me out of her as she gushed all over the counter beneath her. At the same time, Nicole moaned as she came with Tanya from playing with herself as she watched me fuck the daylights out of another woman. With both these women cumming and moaning and screaming in this bathroom stall, I completely lost it, grabbing Tanya's hips and pulling her into me as I shoved my dick one more time as deeply as I could inside her. I came so hard my knees nearly buckled.

As soon as we were all finished cumming on each other, I grabbed the drinks that I had brought with me and passed them out like sticks of gum. Each of us drank them without taking a breath, completely spent from the last few hours with each other. With my dick still inside of Tanya, Nicole came over and reached for the base, gently sliding me out of Tanya and removing the condom. She nudged me to the side so she could lick us both clean, solidifying that we were both hers. She had gotten what she wanted and she wanted both of us to know it.

We cleaned ourselves up and headed out of the bathroom. I kept Tanya's panties in my jacket pocket per Nicole's request. We made sure to exchange numbers with Tanya at the end of the night with promises of "seeing each other" again soon. And as the curtains closed on the night, I had a feeling we'd be seeing much more of Tanya, all right.

Pig Farm

Natalie

Christian and I were newly engaged and living together with a roommate in a small, two-bedroom apartment in New York City, awaiting the end of our lease so we could get our own loft across town. Christian's birthday was quickly approaching and I wanted to do something special for him.

In our entire two years of dating, I had never cooked him a fancy meal because the apartments we both lived in, including the one we now shared together, had kitchens that were just too small. I wanted to go all out with a nice dinner, so I began searching online for a place we could stay for an evening that had the equipment and space I needed.

I found a renovated barn upstate that had a magnificent kitchen. A big, beautiful grey slate island stood in the center. Pots and pans hung over a six-top gas stove from the wide wooden beams that ran across the entire ceiling. The whole place gave off a comfortable, country chic vibe.

The barn-turned-apartment was on a working pig farm, but the price was right and the property so beautiful, its use didn't matter. I booked it immediately, knowing my man would reschedule any prior engagements once I told him I was taking him away overnight.

I packed both of our bags, knowing exactly all we'd need for what I had planned, and we were on our way. Once on the road, I had to make a few stops to grab some necessities, including all the items on my intended menu for each meal. I made Christian stay in the car while I shopped so he wouldn't know what I was up to based on my selections. He helped me put the bags in the trunk and could not stop shaking his head at all of my secrecy.

"What in the world are you up to, girl?" he asked.

I answered his inquiry by not saying a word, just flashing him my biggest smile and winking. As I bent over to put the last of the groceries inside the car, he slapped my ass so hard I immediately yelled, "Owww!" and rubbed right where his big hand had made contact.

As much as it stung, it turned me on more. I attacked him with a huge kiss on the mouth and demanded he stop asking me where we were headed. This man of mine hated to not be in control and just couldn't enjoy a damn surprise!

We got back into the car and as if he knew the results of his playful smack, he put his hand on my leg as I was driving and rubbed up and down my thigh. When I looked over at him and smiled, he moved his hand in between my legs.

He knew I loved it when he was aggressive. I was already wet with excitement over being able to surprise my man; the anticipation of being able to cater to my future husband's every need was driving me crazy. He felt how hot my pussy was through my jeans, and in my head I begged for him to touch me for real.

As if he could read my mind, he undid my button, then took down my zipper and slipped his hand down my pants on top of my panties. What a tease he was! His fingers explored around the top of my pussy and I scooted my ass slightly down my seat so he could get a better feel.

Knowing I was getting hot and bothered, he rested his hand, allowing me to refocus on the road ahead of us. I looked over at him and with a sexy smile purred, "Baby, you're so bad."

Christian, already watching me since he started his little game, responded with, "I'll stop if you want me to."

"I didn't say that!" I pleaded.

He brought his hand up and slipped it underneath my panties. His fingertips softly played with the outer lips of my pussy before moving directly onto my clit. With his index and ring fingers, he spread my pussy open as his middle finger relentlessly flicked on my clit. My juices were puddling underneath me without him even entering me.

Christian

I had never been a big birthday person, but my fiancée was a whole different story. I was getting ahead with work when she came bursting in, bags in hand, a few days before my birthday. She told me to wrap up what I was doing and to clear my schedule for the evening because she was taking me away for my birthday.

What I so loved about this woman was her genuine sense of adventure. From the first day I met her, I realized she had an exploratory spirit that I quickly inherited myself. She made it very clear from the jump that she could not be controlled in a relationship and that she got bored easily. With this woman, I would have to get with it or get lost!

I finished what I was working on and hopped into the shower to get fresh for our latest adventure to God-knew-where this time. With bags already packed, I asked Natalie if there was anything else I needed for the night. With a huge smile on her face, she playfully told me, "Just get your ass in the car, boy!"

As a professional event planner, she loved putting surprises together. She loved the reaction she got from doing things for other people. To see her so joyful inspired a happiness I had never experienced before we met two years ago. Her happiness was truly my happiness, and although I wasn't big on birthdays, to allow her to surprise me was something I would continue to do until the day I died.

We hopped in the car and were on our way. Natalie needed to stop at the grocery store to grab some things for the evening, and of course not wanting to spoil any of the surprise, she made me wait in the car. About twenty minutes later she left the store and I got out to help her put the bags in the trunk. She was being so cute and secretive, an overwhelming urge to smack her hard on the ass came over me.

"Hey!" She squealed and jumped back, massaging the sting away. She glared at me and then leapt into my arms, kissing me deeply.

We finished with the bags and got back on the road. Her energy was so infectious I couldn't keep my hands to myself. I felt her thigh, turning toward her so I could see her every reaction. I had plans of my own for this woman and she had not a clue.

Her pussy was hot under my touch. I undid her zipper

and slid my hand down her pants to grab her whole pussy in my hand. Because she was driving, I decided just to tease her and not give her what I knew she wanted.

She looked over at me. "Baby, you're so bad ..."

I offered to stop. She told me no and I gave her a little more. I brought my hand up and slipped my fingers underneath her panties, finding her clit, which I attacked with my middle finger. She moaned softly at my touch and shook her head at me as I continued to play.

Dripping pussy in hand, I found a rhythm that allowed her to focus on the road and also enjoy the ride as the beautiful scenery surrounded us on all sides. As we drove through a quaint town, I was reminded of the Norman Rockwell paintings that hung in my old barbershop.

At the end of the main street, we turned up a single dirt road and I removed my hand from Nat's pants, as I wanted her yearning for me by the time we reached our destination. We were approaching what looked like a farm, and I couldn't imagine what kind of night Nat had planned for us. I was a city boy and wasn't exactly down for milking any cows or playing with much else except a particular kitty cat.

We parked next to a red barn and Natalie told me, once again, to stay put. She got out of the car to grab the key from the owner. When she opened the door, a mixture of hay and moist soil wafted inside. To my surprise, it smelled fresh to me, not at all what I had expected from a pig farm.

Natalie

After the brutal bout of self-control I had to exercise over the past hour to not to pull over and have Christian take me on the hood of the car, I was relieved to arrive at our destination.

I could tell Christian had no idea where I was taking him by his look of utter confusion as we approached the pig farm I had booked for us.

"I hope you don't expect me to agree that playing around with farm animals is my idea of a fun birthday surprise, Natalie. What are we doing here?"

"Just trust me, it's nothing like that. I'll be right back. Stay here."

As I hopped out of the car to get the keys from Alisa, the property owner, I had to fix my thong that had rode up on me from the drive in. I stuck my hands down the front and back of my jeans to fix it, wiggling it into place, and then zipped my jeans up. As soon as I finished, I looked up and noticed a woman across the road walking toward me. Shit!

I figured it was Alisa, the owner, and slowly started in her direction.

"Natalie?" she called out. I smiled and waved, too embarrassed to speak.

"I'm Alisa, it's great to meet you." She extended her hand for me to shake.

"Nice to meet you too. Natalie." I shook her hand.

"How was your ride in?" She smiled at me knowingly, a gleam in her eye. Dammit, I knew she had seen me fixing myself after I got out of the car. My cheeks flushed crimson.

Alisa was a beautiful and youthful forty-something who totally looked the farmer part. Her messy brown ponytail had hints of natural sun highlighting; she had an angular but feminine face adorned with no makeup. She wore a loose-fitting, denim long-sleeved shirt folded up to the elbows, and dark blue skinny jeans. Her cute sandals suggested she was not going to be getting into any mud in the near future, and being late afternoon, I assumed she was finished working for the day. Something about her was sexy in a very country kind of way.

"Let me help you bring your things inside and I'll show you around a little." She winked.

"OK." I turned around to lead the way. As I approached the car, I realized my palms were sweaty. I silently wondered if it was from the ride in and I hadn't noticed it, or if it was from the thought that Alisa surely knew what Christian and I had been up to. I considered how likely it was that Alisa knew I had rented her spot for the night with the sheer intention of fucking my fiancé all over it.

Christian must have seen us walking toward the car. He opened his door and got out, saying hi to Alisa from across the roof.

"Let's get you two settled."

Christian

What I saw as we headed inside was no barn, but a huge renovated apartment with a modern, spacious kitchen and plush living room area. With eyes wide open, I followed Alisa and Natalie through the entrance and immediately began picturing all the places I'd be fucking my girl later. The kitchen alone was enough to inspire nasty scenes in my head, and I got hard just thinking about what was in store for the next 24 hours.

I knew better than to think Natalie would allow me to get away with watching any TV, but I couldn't help but to check out the large flat-screen TV mounted on the wall with shelves of countless DVDs underneath. Alisa showed Nat the many kitchen appliances as I wandered into the bedroom with its king-sized bed.

"Yeah, she's gonna get it in here tonight," I thought to myself. I threw our bags onto the bed and continued walking to the other end of the room to a door that led to a large bathroom. A huge wooden Jacuzzi sat kitty-corner across from a slate counter with two drop-in sinks. The wall behind the sinks was one massive mirror, and I could already see myself bending Nat over in front of it after a steamy bath in the Jacuzzi, her hands running down the condensation as she reached out for balance.

After giving myself a tour of the place, I could think of nothing else except fucking my wife-to-be, if for no other reason than to show her my love and appreciation. I walked back to the kitchen to find Nat, alone, putting the groceries away.

"Let me help you with that," I growled in her ear as I took the peppers she was holding out of her hand, wrapping my other arm around her waist and pulled her close to me.

As I pushed her forward against the counter, she leaned back against me and tilted her head, exposing her neck so I could suck on it. She pushed her ass back against me and her body responded to my hands running up and down it. After a minute or so, she abruptly took my hands in hers and pried them off of her, discarding them at our sides. She squealed as she broke our embrace and ran around the island away from me.

"No, no, no!" She kept skipping out of reach. "No turning me on. I'm busy," she exclaimed between giggles. We entered a game of cat and mouse, as I played along with her game of trying not to be caught. After a few laps and close calls, I allowed her to win.

"Okay, baby, you win for now, but as soon as I get my hands on you, you're done for!"

She shot me her signature sexy, suggestive look. "Is that so?"

"You're damn right, that's so!"

She clearly was not willing to give it up yet, most likely payback for what I did to her on the ride up. So instead, I ran her a bath and suggested I let her cook in peace while I took a walk into town.

Natalie

The spot was as big and beautiful as the photos I browsed through online before I booked the place. The kitchen was my main focus, and it definitely proved to be up to par with all I had in mind.

"There we go," Alisa stated matter-of-factly as she put down the bags she had in her hands next to the fridge.

"I remember you mentioned in your initial contact to me that the kitchen was what turned you on about the place. It's pretty well-equipped in terms of appliances." As she brought me around the kitchen, she opened different drawers where she pointed out a few appliances I may have had trouble finding. She led me around to the other side of the island and put her hand between two gas range knobs on the stove.

"Make sure you don't try to use these two. They're not dangerous, the pilot flame just doesn't stay on and I haven't had the time to get it fixed. The other four burners should work."

"Okay. So just use these ones."

"Exactly. Also, just so you're aware, and I'm going to

keep him in the house tonight, Skittles, the barn cat, never wastes much time in noticing people are staying here. He's very friendly, but I just wanted to let you know he's around."

I giggled. "That's not a problem. Thank you for the warning, though."

I noticed my palms were sweaty again. I looked around and realized that Christian had wandered into the next room and that Alisa and I were alone once again. I looked back at Alisa.

"If you don't have any questions, I'll leave you to it." She handed me the keys. "I'll be right across the way if you need anything."

"Cool. Thank you so much for everything. If we need anything, I'll let you know." And with that, she turned to go.

I watched her to the door, checking her out as she walked away. Farming sure did a body good; I could see the muscle definition on her petite frame.

As soon as she closed the door, I began to put the groceries away. The food had endured an hour-plus car ride and needed to be put away as soon as possible.

After Christian was finished exploring the place, I felt his presence behind me. I loved that he was always up to no good and couldn't keep his hands off me, but he was going to have to wait after all the delicious teasing he put me through on the drive in.

As he pressed his body against my backside, he removed the food in my hand and pushed me forward against the counter. I gasped slightly, surprised at his sudden aggression, and then smiled to myself. I had this man right where I wanted him. He was not going to get this pussy as easily as he did in the car.

I leaned back against his warm body, relaxing, as I let my head fall back on his shoulder, enticing him to kiss my exposed neck. Of course he bit at my bait, pun intended, and I moved my body back against him, undoubtedly leading him to believe I had become putty in his hands.

His hands, with a desperate urgency, felt up and down my body; from my perky breasts, down my sides, to the front of my body; to the front of my thighs and in between my legs and back up again. I placed my hands on top of his, allowing his hands to lead mine all over. He moved his body against mine in unison and just as my pussy grew wet again, I took his hands and threw them off me, escaping his grip.

I ran around to the other side of the island and stopped, looking at him, inviting him to chase me. He appeased me for a few laps, eventually giving up. As if he knew what I was up to, he offered to draw me a bath and get lost for a few.

The water was the perfect temperature, as only Christian seemingly knew how to run it. The barn came equipped with the freshest scented bath oils and soaps, handmade on this very farm. Reading the label, I slowly untied the twine as my thoughts wandered to Alisa carefully choosing the fresh herbs and oils used to create the soap I was about to cleanse myself with. Her hands, the same strong hands used for raising livestock and harvesting crops, tactfully mixing all her ingredients together. I put those thoughts aside.

I stripped down to nothing and stared at my naked curves in the full-length mirror, pleased with my progress in the gym. I was thankful Christian had gone for a walk, leaving me to wash up and take care of myself before the evening was in full swing. I exfoliated my entire body and shaved myself bald from nose to toes. I then laid back and touched myself, allowing my thoughts to travel to the pounding I was due as soon as I gave in to my man, while the jets from the Jacuzzi massaged my lower back. I couldn't wait to feel his thick shaft against my clit before he slid it all the way deep inside me.

Just then, I heard a knock on the door.

"Oh, shit!" I thought. "Christian can't be back already, he just left."

"Hello?" I called out.

I heard a woman's voice call my name and recognized her as Alisa, the property owner. I turned off the jets of the Jacuzzi.

My thoughts immediately turned to Christian. Maybe she had seen him leaving and thought we had a fight and he had walked out on me. Did she see something happen to him? I began to panic slightly—what if he's hurt? Alisa would sound far more urgent had there been anything wrong. Maybe she was just checking in. But wouldn't it have been a lot less creepy to ring the doorbell? Was this even legal? I decided it best to just figure out once and for all what the reason was for this woman knocking.

A shadow appeared beneath the bathroom door. "Hi Nat, I just wanted to check on you guys and make sure you had everything you needed ..." she said, her face close to the door.

A wave of relief washed over me. Christian was okay. She was just checking on us. Or checking on me ...

The question still remained whether or not she had seen Christian leave for his walk. A different type of concern now consumed me. Perhaps I had seen one too many horror movies, but I was almost certain a woman naked and alone in a barn she rented for herself and her boyfriend for the night was the perfect setting for a blood bath. A voice interrupted the scene in my head of my own body floating dead in this very bathtub, the water a deep red.

"If you don't need anything, I'm going to turn in for the night ..."

"OK. She's offering to leave," my internal dialogue continued. "That's a good sign. I think." Suddenly, I was overcome with a novel emotion.

I had a decision to make. Either make a fuss about the intrusion—the nerve of this woman entering the house we had paid to have our privacy in!—or extend her the invitation to come all the way into a most private moment.

My mind wandered to our previous interaction while alone as she showed me around the kitchen. I couldn't help but to think she was ... flirting? There was no doubt in my mind she had an idea of what happened on our drive in ... could she perhaps want a little of that action as well? I privately prayed she was still standing outside the door.

"Come in." My voice was barely audible. The ball was out of my court. If she was still there and could hear my call, it was up to her to answer it. If she had already left, then so be it. Again, I prayed.

Silence from the other side returned my call. The anticipation I felt just moments before deflated like a helium balloon. Then, slowly and soundlessly, the door opened. Rather than reach for a towel or washcloth, or question the intrusion, I maintained my position in the tub, legs splayed. My excitement returned.

As I saw Alisa come from around the door, my pussy pulsated. The bubbles from the Jacuzzi jets had settled and the soap suds were the only things standing between my naked body and Alisa's gaze. She didn't pretend to ignore what was happening underneath the water as I carried on touching myself.

Finally, Alisa offered the explanation for her entrance: she had been having trouble finding Skittles, and wanted to make sure, before it got too late in the evening, that she located him. She hadn't gotten a response when she knocked on the door.

"I hope I'm not disrupting you," she added, more polite than apologetic.

"Disrupting … no." I chose my words wisely.

She tilted her chin up a bit and moved her head forward just slightly. A movement to let me know she was peeking at what was going on beneath the surface.

My fingers continued to make small circles on my clit. The array of emotions the last few minutes elicited had heightened my sensitivity, that was for sure.

Alisa was in no rush to leave the bathroom and I was in no hurry to see her go. After a long while of us staring at each other, she finally drawled, "I trust you'll let me know if you need anything while you're here."

"I will," I promised. "Thanks, Alisa."

At that she smiled and turned to go.

"I want to thank you for your hospitality ..." I mumbled, knowing that wasn't what I wanted to thank her for.

"You have a really beautiful property," I added, feeling more cowardly by the second.

She turned to face me, knowing something was up, as who would have expected me to say such normal words under such a nasty setting?

She looked directly into my eyes and urged me, "Just say it."

I looked deeply into her eyes, and with my cheeks red as the barn, whispered what I really wanted to thank her for ...

"Thank you, Alisa, for turning me on as I touch myself to the sight of you standing there. You are quite the visual stimulation ..."

She unbuttoned the denim shirt she wore to expose her hard nipples and perfectly plump breasts. She walked over toward me and flipped the switch on the jets.

"Position yourself against the bubbles. I want to watch you cum."

I erupted before she even finished her sentence.

A victorious grin played across her lips. As I caught my breath, I silently wondered if Skittles was really missing or if Alisa had just seen Christian leave for his walk and wanted to catch me alone. Either way, it didn't matter now, as I sat in the warm water, delighted that that gentle knock on the door not only made me cum, but that I didn't end up in a pool of my own blood. Shit, Christian!

Alisa must have seen the realization on my face while I sat up in the tub as it dawned on me that this turned out to be a much longer bath than expected; he'd probably be back any minute.

"Looks like the original kitty I was looking for isn't in here. I should get going." Alisa flashed a quick smile and was gone as abruptly as she came.

Reluctantly, I got out of the tub, toweled off and headed naked to the bedroom where Christian had brought our bags. It was the first time I had really gotten to see the place, and it was simply breathtaking. Everything was so clean and crisp, but comfy and inviting all at the same time.

I had brought with me an array of lingerie to cook in,

and a few pairs of my favorite stilettos to match each outfit. I slipped into an all-black, lacy set and my comfiest four-inch pumps and got to work. I started by putting out the handmade menus I made yesterday and prepped the food.

Just as I was finishing cutting the vegetables, Christian walked in.

"Oh man, baby, this place is so worth seeing. Maybe after dinner we'll take a long walk. You've got to see this place!"

"I'm glad you enjoyed, baby." I pointed to the bedroom. "Now get your fine ass in the shower so I can feed you already."

He came over to where I was standing and took my ass in both of his hands, pulling me into him and kissing me.

"I hope you're on the menu, otherwise I may just hold off and make you dessert."

I smiled against his lips and kissed him back. "I promise dinner will be worth it, then I have something special for you for dessert. Now go clean up, baby!" I demanded.

He begged me to join him, which I had to decline even though I so wanted to get busy with this man. He finally let go of me and stripped on his way out of the kitchen. As he dropped his shirt to the floor, his chiseled back was in plain view, with his briefs peeking out from his pants. Damn, this man of mine was so fine.

He came out a little while later smelling like cologne and the homemade bath soap I had used myself that Alisa made. Oh, Alisa! I had been so focused on preparing dinner for Christian I hadn't even thought about what had happened earlier in that same bathroom.

If I told him about our episode before dinner, he would

never let us eat, excited to know every detail, and he would definitely no longer take no for an answer from me. Perhaps I would incorporate the juicy details into the special dessert I had planned for him ...

Christian

The warm May air felt great as I headed out to explore the area. There weren't as many animals in sight for what I would have expected for a farm. True to its title, there were indeed pigs, but the renovations Alisa had done on the barn explained the lack of larger animals that would have needed the shelter.

The smell of the pigs was interesting, to say the least. I had smelled cow manure once while driving to a retreat, but this was something entirely different. It was a smell I could have gone my life without smelling. Luckily, the pigpens were far enough from the road that it wasn't too obnoxious.

The property looked to be a few acres, but the barn was close to the entrance, so it wasn't long before I was headed to town. I figured Nat wouldn't need more than an hour or so to bathe and prep dinner, so I decided I would only walk for about thirty minutes before I turned around and headed back.

All I kept thinking as I walked around was, "Nat would love this," and "Nat would love that!"

She was born and raised in a small town and although she always says she is a city girl at heart, I know she innately enjoys the country; after all, she brought us to a farm. The more I thought about her, the more I missed her, and so I decided to head back early. I grabbed a big bouquet of flowers to decorate the kitchen island with and was on my way.

As I approached the barn, even over the pungent smell

of the pigs I could already smell the delicious scent coming from inside. Nat always said how much she wanted to cook a full dinner for me, fantasizing about our future home with a large kitchen, so I knew tonight's meal was going to be on point.

Nat had on this sexy black number, tits sitting all high, nipples showing through the lace that was more aesthetic than functional, her ass as plump as ever, exposed around a thin lace thong that sat high on her hips, legs bare and hairless ending in a pair of simple black patent leather pumps.

I walked right up to her after setting down the flowers and grabbed her ass with both my hands, pulling her toward me. This woman surely knew how to tease the shit out of a man, and I could hardly stand it any longer! I pleaded with her to join me when she directed me to take a shower, knowing my efforts would likely be futile. I knew she was full swing in the middle of dinner, but I figured it was worth a try.

I headed toward the bathroom slowly, taking off my shirt as I went, thinking, "Two can play at this game."

The hot water felt good running down my body, but my hunger quickly took over, both for dinner and for my wife to-be. I washed up, threw on a pair of gray sweats and returned to the kitchen.

Nat directed me to a chair at the island. "Sit right there, baby. Dinner will be ready shortly, and then we can finally eat."

I complied.

The view of my girl wearing close to nothing in those heels gave hunger a whole new meaning. She was facing away from me at the sink, her ass jiggling slightly with every move she made. As I stared at her body, all hunger for food disappeared, and this woman in front of me became my sole focus. I got hard just thinking about bending her over the sink, ripping her bra off and letting her tits bounce around in the soapy water as I fucked her hard from the back.

She looked back at me over her shoulder as she dropped a spoon, waking me from my daydream. Keeping her eyes on mine, she slowly bent over, arching her back and keeping her legs straight so her hips widened and her fat pussy lips hung down in between her round, plump ass. My dick was standing at full attention and I stroked it.

The yoga classes she had been taking were clearly paying off as she bent all the way to the floor to retrieve the spoon without bending her knees in those heels. I could see she was soaking wet through her panties and I nearly lost it. I wanted her so bad.

She stood up as slowly as she bent over, maintaining eye contact with me the whole time. She moved from the sink to the stove and slowly stirred the sauce she had simmering. She removed the spoon and fed herself a taste. She looked pleased and let out an affirmative moan of satisfaction. She shifted her weight as she replaced the spoon and then brought it around to pour the red sauce down the back of her ass. She looked at me again, this time with a sly smile dancing on her lips. Her eyes begged me to come closer.

"Baby, you seem to have spilled some," I teased.

"Oh did, I?" she responded playfully. "I hadn't noticed. Where, baby?" She took the spoon and poured more sauce down her ass, letting it drip down the back of her leg.

"Where?" I echoed as I got off my chair and kneeled down behind her. "Right ... here ... baby." I licked the sauce off in between each word. I reached around to grip the front of her legs as I licked from the bottom of her legs all the way up to her ass. I slowly licked her ass clean as my hands explored all over her hips and thighs. I hooked my thumbs in the straps of her thong and slowly slid it down to the floor.

I reached under her from the back, grabbing a handful of pussy as I bit her ass hard. The pain mixed with pleasure stood her up on her tippy toes and she squealed like the pigs outside.

"Baby!" she exclaimed.

With her juices all over my hand, I said, "That's payback for all this waiting you're making me do!"

I moved my fingers around on her clit as my other hand gripped her thigh to steady her. I pulled her hips back as I slipped my fingers into her dripping wet pussy and stuck my tongue right between her ass cheeks. I was not about to let her go after getting my dick so hard with her little sauce routine.

She let out a gasp before reaching back to spread her ass wide open for me as she bent forward onto the counter beside the stove. She loved having her ass eaten more than any woman I had ever been with. I loved anything that brought her pleasure.

With her torso on the counter, I pulled my fingers out of her and forced her legs as far apart as possible, giving me better access to stick my entire face between her legs. I moved my tongue up and down, licking from her ass all the way to her clit and back again, over and over in a nodding motion.

She moaned and her breath quickened. I made small circles on her anus before I pressed two fingers deep into her ass. She let out one final moan before yelling, "Baby, I'm gonna cum!" She gushed all over my face and down her legs, making a puddle on the floor underneath us.

Before she was even able to catch her breath, I stood behind her and finally, with my dick in my hand, shoved it hard into her dripping pussy. I gripped her hips as she grabbed the edge of the counter, and I punished her for making me wait so damn long.

I slowed down enough to grab the spoon from the pot of sauce and poured the hot sauce all the way down her spine tattoo and onto her ass. I pulled out of her and from her ass all the way up her tattoo, I cleaned the sauce off with my tongue before ramming my dick inside her ass so I could bust inside it. With her ass popping on my dick, I got closer to cumming. As though we had planned it, I busted inside her just as the timer went off, signaling dinner was ready.

Natalie

Christian returned from the shower smelling like a piece of heaven, and I directed him to sit near me so he would have a front-row seat to what I was about to do. As I maneuvered around the kitchen, his eyes burned holes through me. I had just put chicken in the oven to bake, so we had at least thirty minutes before it'd be ready.

Standing in front of the stove, I stirred the sauce my mother had taught me how to make as a little girl, cooling it enough to use in a way Mama might not approve of. I took a taste—it was the best I had ever made.

I took the spoonful of sauce, leaned forward and poured the sauce directly onto my ass. While it burned slightly where it landed, I was pleased as it dripped all the way down my leg. I smiled at Christian when he mentioned I spilled some. I played stupid and poured more sauce down the other leg. Covered in sauce, I asked him if he could point out where I had spilled.

He got up off his chair and onto his hands and knees behind me. With his tongue tracing all up and down my legs, I shivered from the hot sauce contrasting the coolness from his breath as he cleaned me up. The sensation of his soothing tongue licking where the heat from the sauce stung felt incredible, and I soaked through my panties. When he was done cleaning up the sauce, he slid my panties down to my ankles.

His hands traveled back up the insides of my thighs and right up to grab my pussy. I felt his hot breath on my ass, and then he bit down hard, causing me to scream.

"Baby!" I looked down over my shoulder at him.

"That's payback for all this waiting you're making me do!"

I rolled my eyes at him as he made small circles on my clit before sliding his fingers inside me. I could hardly stay mad for long. As if to apologize, he pulled my hips back and stuck his tongue in my ass. I leaned forward onto the counter for balance and reached back to grab my cheeks to spread them so he could go deeper. There was nothing I loved more than a little booty play.

I was beginning to lose track of how many times my legs almost failed me on these four-inch stilettos. My entire body was shaking. He replaced his fingers with his tongue as he licked from my ass to my clit. My pussy exploded when he pushed two fingers inside my ass, creating a puddle on the floor.

The buildup from the car ride, to the bathtub incident with Alisa and now this latest attack with the sauce was too much to handle. I had to feel my man's big dick inside my tight little pussy. As if he could read my mind, he stood, steadied himself with his hands on my hips and slammed his dick deep inside me repeatedly. This was definitely payback for all the teasing I had put him through all day.

He slowed his pace and then a burning sensation traveled down my spine and onto my ass. Christian then pulled out of me and licked all the way from my ass up my entire back, before pushing his dick deep inside my ass.

He found his pace and I threw my ass back at him until he could take it no longer and let go inside me. It was so sexy to have my man react so immediately to my body, and we both collapsed on top of each other on the counter. Just as he came, the timer for the chicken went off. We let the buzzer ring as we caught our breath together.

Finally Christian stood, pulled out of me, and went to turn off the timer. I found my legs again and stood, still unsteady from the beating. I had no more use for my heels and kicked them off to finish preparing our plates as Christian cleaned up the floor from all the mess we made before washing his hands.

We finally sat down to eat, both so hungry we barely said a word. As we finished eating, Christian babbled about God knows what, but I couldn't hear a word he was saying because my head was swirling with thoughts of Alisa and how I was going to tell my man of our bathroom episode.

I knew he wouldn't be upset, but I also didn't want to just blurt it out. I considered telling him all the sexy details between licks of him while on my knees for dessert, but I wanted his undivided attention without distractions. Instead, as soon as we finished eating, I stood up and pushed our plates aside with one sweep, making so much noise I got Christian's attention, all right.

"Nat, what are you doing?"

I hoisted myself up on the counter in front of him. I leaned forward and took his face in my hands and kissed him softly on the lips before looking him directly in the eyes.

"Baby, I want to share something with you that happened when you went for a walk ..."

"Okay ..." He narrowed his eyes, unsure where I was headed.

"It's Alisa." I paused, eyeing him expectantly for a reaction.

"Alisa ... go on."

"Well, when I was taking a bath, there was a knock at the door and it was her. At first I thought something might have happened to you, but she didn't sound concerned."

Christian sat motionless, listening. I continued.

"She couldn't have known I was taking a bath, but she let herself in anyways. She said she was trying to find the cat and didn't get an answer when she knocked at the front door. Honestly, I think that part is bullshit; I think she saw you leave and wanted to get me alone."

He shrugged and lifted his eyebrows at the possibility.

"Ever since I grabbed the keys from her, there's been a vibe between us. I didn't really figure out what it was until she came into the bathroom. I was playing with myself, fantasizing about pulling over on our ride here and fucking you on the side of the highway. When she came in, I didn't stop."

Again I paused, expecting a reaction. Christian just sat there, taking in my every word. I continued.

"Baby, it turned me on ... her standing there watching

me play with myself under the soapy water. I was nervous at first to admit it, and then I came so hard after I got the courage to tell her. She kept repeatedly offering to let her know if we needed anything. And then she left."

As soon as I was finished, my pussy soaking wet again at my recollection, Christian had one question for me.

"Do you want her?"

I was shy to answer yes, but I couldn't deny how I felt. Christian already knew the answer and would know I was lying anyway, so I came clean.

"I do, baby, and I want her with you."

"Well then, you know what we have to do."

His words and the lust on his face instantly made my pussy start throbbing. As innocent as I could be, this man knew and expected how easily I found trouble everywhere I went.

"What's that?"

He leaned forward and stuck his tongue deep into my mouth. He stood up in between my legs, spread them apart and with no hesitation or delay, eased his hard dick inside my pussy once more. I moaned deeply against his mouth and bit his lip as he pulled away from my face. It concerned me slightly that he hadn't answered my question.

He looked me in my eyes, fucking me deeply and slowly. "Thank you for telling me about Alisa, baby. You have no idea how much your honesty means to me."

He slowed his pace even further and gave me a devilish grin. "Let's get her, baby." With one hand behind my back for support, he leaned forward toward me and pushed one of the plates onto the floor, smashing the porcelain all over the tile. I looked at him, surprised, and without having to say a word, he answered my question.

"Let's see if we can get her to come back."

With those words, I exploded all over his dick as he quickened his pace to match the throbbing of my pussy walls. As soon as I finished cumming, he slowed his pace slightly.

"The mere thought of Alisa makes you cum, huh, baby?" he said as his dick was going deep inside me over and over.

I so loved when this man talked shit to me. "I wanna taste what Alisa does to you."

He slammed his dick as hard as he could inside me and then pulled out of me and dropped to his knees in front of me. I lay back onto the counter, knocking another plate to the floor, making an even louder crash on the already broken plate below. Christian stuck his tongue deep inside my pussy, sucking and slurping the cum from my Alisa orgasm.

Our plan must have worked because within minutes, I heard a faint door creaking. I sat up on my elbows and looked down at Christian, who didn't miss a beat on my pussy. He was too deep inside me to hear a noise so quiet, and it turned me on that once again, Alisa and I shared a naughty secret.

Alisa crept silently across the room toward where my man was eating me out right on top of her island counter in front of her. I smiled to myself at the thought of getting caught getting busy in someone else's kitchen. As Alisa approached, she unbuttoned her blouse, inviting me for a second look at her perfect rack. My pussy throbbed at the memory of the first time she exposed herself to me.

She walked around to the other side of the island, opposite the broken plates, stepping each leg out of her jeans as she came closer. She quietly climbed onto the countertop next to me, and on her hands and knees, crawled closer so her face was hovering above mine. Christian couldn't see anything, tongue-deep in my pussy. Alisa bent her arms, lowering herself, and stuck her tongue all the way in my mouth. Her lips were full and soft, and her tongue tasted like sweet raspberries.

My pussy throbbed from the kiss I had been so looking forward to. With my tongue swirling chaotically and passionately around Alisa's, and Christian's tongue fucking my pussy, I moaned intensely into Alisa's mouth. Christian stopped immediately. He knew me well enough that even the slightest change in the pitch or volume of my moans alerted him.

He retracted his tongue from my pussy and circled my clit, surely sneaking a peek at what had caused the change. A low moan escaped his mouth, vibrating on my clit. Knowing full well what I was up to, he slowly kissed my inner thigh, up to my knee, so he could get a full view. My heart beat faster at the thrill of Christian witnessing the hunger I had for Alisa.

Christian

Nat and I were so hungry after our sexual appetizer that we ate in silence and were finished in no time. After years of hearing about Natalie's cooking skills, she did not disappoint. Every bite mixed with the delicious sauce reminded me of Nat's full-on sauce assault. I sat through the entire dinner with my dick hard. I was relieved to see Nat eating as quickly as I was, because I couldn't wait to have her again for dessert.

When my mouth was finally empty, I tried conversation, but Nat interrupted me, shoving the dishes aside with a loud clatter. She positioned herself in front of me on the table and told me she had something to tell me. The concern on her face alarmed me; something was bothering her.

To my utter shock, she dove into a story about the bath I had run for her earlier and how none other than the property owner, Alisa, barged in on her. Nat told me how she came as Alisa talked dirty to her to get her off! It shouldn't have surprised me, considering trouble followed Natalie in the most unsuspecting of situations.

As I sat and listened to this story of my girl and this other woman, my head swirled with possibility. Perhaps I'd be getting more than I bargained for with this evening getaway. When she was finished talking, I had one question. I asked Nat if she wanted Alisa. Hesitantly, she admitted she did. No doubt Alisa had a thing for my girl, as well, or she wouldn't have intruded.

Suddenly, an idea came to mind. With Alisa being so close in proximity, perhaps loud noise would draw her back. She clearly knew no boundaries and took the phrase "owns the place" literally, so I decided to put it to the test. With confirmation that my girl was interested, I stood up, grabbed the base of my hard dick and pushed it all the way deep into Nat's pussy. I kissed her and thanked her for her honesty.

"Let's get her, baby!" I challenged as I reached behind her and slid a plate crashing to the floor.

The loud noise made Nat's muscles contract around my dick as she let out a little gasp. Her eyes widened as she looked at me dead in the face.

Amused, I offered, "Let's see if we can get Alisa to come back."

With that, Nat came hard all over my dick, gripping and scratching at my biceps as she let go. That the simple mention of another woman's name made Natalie cum on command was so hot. This was new territory.

I wanted to taste what the thought of this woman did to my girl. I pulled out of her and got on my knees so I could stick my tongue deep inside her pussy and suck out all her cum.

Nose deep in Nat's pussy, her juices dripping down my chin and leaking down her ass, her moans became muffled. Her cries of pleasure turned to distracted, muted moans. I quickly moved my devouring tongue up to her clit to see if perhaps my plan worked and Alisa had responded to the noise.

The first thing I saw was two sets of tits. I smiled; the plate trick had worked. Natalie was tonguing down the owner of the barn, who had watched my girl explode in the tub mere hours ago. I kissed and sucked my way up Natalie's thigh as my hands ran up her hips and onto her tits. I stood; it was the first time I really paid any attention to Alisa. The first impression I formed when I met her vanished, replaced with the description of the scene in the bathroom. Looking at her, it didn't surprise me how Natalie could be attracted to her. Alisa was smokin'.

Alisa was the first to pull away. She continued to stare down at Nat as she wiggled out of her panties using one hand and let them fall to the floor. She must have stripped the rest of her clothes while I was busy tasting the orgasm this woman prompted. She looked over at me, and with a devilish grin like she'd just gotten away with something, she crawled toward me. Before she stuck her tongue all the way into my mouth, she looked at Nat with her eyebrow raised, and Nat nodded with a sexy smile. Alisa tongued me down like I was a meal and she hadn't eaten in days. She put her hands around the back of my neck to steady herself and then slowly lifted and placed her leg on the other side of Nat, straddling her reverse-cowgirl style.

Natalie

Alisa slowly sucked on my lower lip as she broke out of our kiss. She looked me dead in the face as she reached down to slide her panties off, steadying herself above me with her other hand. I lifted my head slightly to see Christian standing, staring as Alisa slowly slid her panties off over her ass. She lifted each knee to free them from under her, her body rocking slightly forward, her nipples just inches from my mouth. I wanted so badly to lift my head to suck on them, but like Christian, I was transfixed.

Alisa sat up and looked over at Christian. She looked back at me, a glance that silently asked permission to let the night take us wherever it was meant to go. I smiled and nodded back to her, not knowing I had just sealed our fate of a wild ride.

She crawled across the counter over to Christian and shoved her tongue down his throat. The sight of my man kissing another woman turned me on, and as I reached down toward my pussy, Alisa got on top of me backward, giving me a front-row seat to her plump, luscious ass. She leaned forward to tongue my man down harder and I grabbed her hips to steady her so she could really go at him. Sitting on me the way she did, her hips spread out, making her ass look twice as big and her already tiny waist even smaller.

I massaged the crease where the top of her thigh met her body and rubbed all over her hips. With her back arched, I spread her cheeks open as wide as they could go to reveal her pretty little pussy, which was already glistening in anticipation.

I reached my hand under her to cup her pussy and spread her lips with my fingers, getting her juices all over my hand. As I rubbed her wetness all over her clit, I felt the same movement on my own. I was so wet I couldn't tell if it was my man's hand or Alisa's hand, and I didn't really care.

Just as I got ready to stick a finger in Alisa's pussy, I felt a pressure on my own pussy, as Christian's dick pushed deep inside me with one hard thrust. I let out a scream that was equally pleasure and surprise. I slid two fingers inside Alisa as my man pounded me harder and harder until I reached my climax and screamed out. He continued to fuck me, splashing my cum all over.

Christian slowed his pace and started fucking me with a jackhammer, all the way in and then pulling all the way out, the head of his dick gently rubbing up my clit each time before sliding back inside me. Alisa sat up straight and began to move back and forth, riding my fingers that were still inside her. I could feel Alisa's fingers on my clit every time Christian's dick went inside me. The sensation of his hard dick hitting the bottom of my pussy and the constant rubbing on my clit made me squirt all over.

Christian

With Alisa facing me backward on top of Nat, her hands still around my neck, I stared intently at her face. It was like watching a movie of the facial progression of her growing more and more horny. She arched her back as she closed her eyes, her chin tilting toward the sky. She opened her eyes and grabbed the base of my dick with one hand and began to rub it up and down Nat's slippery pussy.

Alisa made my dick nice and wet before holding it at the entrance. I leaned forward and pushed it all the way deep inside Nat. She let out a scream that made Alisa smile in satisfaction. Nat's breath quickened and I could feel her walls contract around me as she nutted all over my dick. As I continued to fuck Nat, Alisa began to move her hips back and forth, her tits bouncing with every thrust. Alisa put one hand on Nat's thigh as the other rubbed her clit. She squirted again.

After both girls were thoroughly drenched in Nat's juices, Alisa backed away from me. I could see she wanted in on the action.

She looked me dead in the eye. "I want to taste what you do to your girl, what I saw her do to herself in the tub before."

I stood there speechless. This chick may have wanted my girl just as much as I did, and it didn't seem as if she'd be taking no for an answer. All I could do was nod yes and try to keep my jaw from dropping to the ground.

She smiled and proceeded to inch herself backward, rubbing her pussy up Nat's torso until her pink pussy lips were dangling right over Nat's mouth. I backed away enough to bend down to see Nat's tongue stick straight up to catch the juices dripping from Alisa's pussy.

Alisa shoved her pussy down onto Nat's face and laid herself on top of her so she could taste the cum and squirt juices I'd created. Still standing back, with my rock-hard dick standing straight out, I touched myself at the beautiful sight in front of me: my girl and the owner 69-ing right where my girl and I ate dinner just moments before.

As I got harder and harder thinking about how I was the luckiest man alive, Alisa reached out and grabbed my dick to pull me closer. She pulled me close enough to take my dick and rub it between Nat's soaking wet pussy lips, making sure to rub the head on her ass, too; she rubbed it from her ass up to her clit and back again.

She then looked up at me, smiled, and opened her mouth wide, nodding at me as if to say, "I want to feel you in the back of my throat." Without hesitation, I shoved my hard dick all the way into Alisa's mouth, gagging her and making her whole body tighten.

She kept her mouth open wide and stuck her tongue out, gagging each time I slammed my dick down her throat until she pushed me away. I stepped toward her again and this time she took my dick in her hand once more.

She looked up at me. "I want to suck on her pussy while you take her ass. Can you make that happen?"

"You got it, girl."

She smiled at me, looked back down and rubbed the head of my dick in small circles around Nat's anus. She spit on it and Nat began to moan loudly; Alisa had no idea the gold she had struck. Alisa grabbed the base and pushed me gently inside. It only took a few seconds for my dick to work itself all the way in. Between the cum, the squirt, and the spit, Nat's ass was nice and ready for me. Once I found my rhythm, Alisa leaned her head back down and smooshed her face into Nat's pussy, coming up only for air as she watched my big dick go in and out of my girl's tight ass.

Natalie

The weight of Alisa's tight little body inched along me, leaving a trail of pussy juice all the way up my torso. Her ass got bigger and more beautiful the closer it got until her pussy lips hung above my face. I lifted my head and stuck my tongue out and up into Alisa's pussy. She tasted so sweet.

Not a beat later, I felt Alisa's tongue flick on my clit. In that moment of ecstasy, I was so grateful she'd been nosy enough to enter that bathroom while I was playing with myself earlier. To have this stranger's sweet pussy in my face and her mouth sucking the life out of me turned me on incredibly. I had finally and fully embraced Alisa's offer of assistance. I wondered if this is what she had meant all along.

The feeling of Christian's hard dick rubbing up and down my pussy disrupted my thoughts. I could feel Alisa guiding it from my ass to my clit. Suddenly, Alisa's body contracted on top of me and I could hear her gag on Christian's dick. Hearing her slurping and gasping got my pussy throbbing again as I pictured Christian fucking Alisa's face. I stuck my fingers in her pussy and pushed deep inside her every time Christian's dick pushed her backward. Together we fucked her from both ends.

I heard her gasp for breath one final time, then I felt pressure against my ass. Christian's dick made small circles around and around and I heard Alisa spit. Then, slowly, she guided Christian's thick dick deeper and deeper into my ass. Once Christian worked it to the base, I felt Alisa's tongue on my clit and I almost lost it. The two of them gained momentum in tandem as I laid my head back on the counter. There was no way in hell I was going to be able to focus on pleasing Alisa now.

I tried to keep my legs from shaking uncontrollably as Alisa inched her way closer to the action, giving me the most perfect view of her ass. Her pussy was swollen with pleasure and I watched it drip onto my chest. She obviously was enjoying the sight of Christian's dick going in and out of my ass. I used the wetness to rub on my nipples.

Christian began to pick up his pace, his dick having stretched my ass out enough so that there was no pain whatsoever. Alisa's entire body began to shake until she could no longer focus on pleasing me and exploded all over me, watching my man fuck my ass at such close range.

Out of breath, she lay her face against the inside of my thigh. She began to rub my clit with her fingers as Christian fucked me faster and faster. Alisa then shoved two fingers inside my pussy and flicked my G-spot while licking my clit at the same time, begging me to finish. Her soft tongue on my most sensitive spot, her fingers inside my pussy and my man claiming my ass all at the same time sent me over the edge.

As my heart raced and my pussy pulsated, Christian's breath quickened as he let go in my ass, keeping his dick deep inside me. He slowly pulled out and Alisa licked me clean.

Christian collapsed on the nearest chair as I caught my breath, the weight of Alisa still on top of me. Slowly, she worked her way off me and lay on her back right next to where I lay. No one spoke a word.

As we all took a moment to catch our breath, a quiet scratching came from the other side of a door I hadn't noticed before. I turned my head and looked at Alisa. She glanced over at me before sitting up abruptly.

"Skittles!" She jumped up off the counter and hurried over to open the door.

"There you are, dummy!" She bent over and picked up the small gray cat, holding him against her bare chest.

She came over to where I was now sitting on the

counter, butt naked and exhausted.

"So this is the little guy who started all of this," I teased, extending my hand for Skittles to sniff. He licked my fingers.

"That was him, all right. And it seems as though he likes the taste of you, too." She smiled at me then lowered her chin and kissed him on top of his head.

"Back to where you belong, now. Let's leave these two alone."

She walked over to the bedroom door and closed it before dropping Skittles on the ground. Christian had gotten up to gather Alisa's clothes. She pulled her pants on first and I helped her button up her blouse, taking one final opportunity to get a close look at her perfect tits. She lifted my chin as I buttoned her last button and kissed me.

"From the second you got out of the car, fixing yourself from the ride up ..." She paused and smiled, which made me laugh out loud. "I had to see for myself what your man already had." I blushed crimson yet again.

"Thank you for inviting me in today, in every way." She kissed me again on the mouth. "And I'll continue to say it till I'm blue in the face: if you need anything, let me know." She beamed a big smile at me.

She turned to face Christian. "And thank you as well, for sharing. I know it's your birthday weekend, but I couldn't help myself. Happy birthday to all of us, I guess!"

We all laughed as she scooped up Skittles. She walked toward the front door and opened it. She looked back at us over her shoulder. "I hope to see you guys soon." And with that, Alisa and Skittles disappeared into the night.

Blind Toys

Evan

My wife, Kat, and I celebrated our seven-year anniversary right before a couple of mutual friends announced their engagement. They had been together for a decade, so they planned on having the wedding within three months. Despite having lived the married life for quite some time, they both made sure to have the proper bachelor and bachelorette celebrations, the latter of which Kat was expected to return from this evening. The girls flew out to Vegas for the week, and I was fully expecting to hear all about the wild time they had.

We had been asked to housesit for a few friends of ours who left for a summer vacation getaway, and so we had this massive mansion all to ourselves for the next week. While Kat was still away in Vegas, I was able to get familiar with the house in a way I had never been able to during the dinner parties our friends would throw often.

The girls arranged for a car service to grab them from the airport and drop them off at their respective homes. She texted me when she landed and I sent her the exact address of the house. While Kat was on her way, I ran to the store to grab some items in preparation for her arrival, and then sat down to relax while my favorite basketball team kicked some ass.

With perfect timing, Kat walked through the door during a commercial toward the end of the game. She dropped her bags at the front door and gave me a passionate kiss hello, an obvious glow surrounding her.

"Hi, my love," she said as she pulled away.

"Hi, baby." I squeezed her ass and smiled. "How was your week?"

"Oh my God, it was crazy. Ashley is literally insane!" She rolled her eyes dramatically and stepped out of my arms.

I had no idea what she meant.

"Well, I know that already. I assume she pulled out all the stops for herself?" I bent down to grab her bags, noticing she had come back with more than she had left with for the week. I headed up the stairs.

"Of course she did!" Kat shook her head, following me to the master bedroom. "It was definitely everything you could imagine a bachelorette party in Vegas to be!"

"Well I'm glad you enjoyed yourself. I know they say 'What happens in Vegas stays in Vegas,' but if you want to spill, I'm all ears." I winked at her.

"Sure," she said, kissing me again. "I'm going to hop in the shower and then I'll tell you all about it!"

I let Kat get settled in and went back to the living room to catch the end of the game. My team was up by a basket with two minutes left, which was too close for comfort, considering how much grief I'd get at work if they lost. A few of the guys in the office and I had a huge fan rivalry and often put money on games. I desperately needed a win to save face in the midst of all the shit talking I'd been doing that week. Just as the clock was winding down in the last minute of the game, Kat came out and stood in front of the TV.

"Baby, you're in the way," I pleaded, not focused on anything aside from a win.

She didn't move. I scooted over on the couch so I could see the screen and she took a step to the side, blocking my view once more. She was wearing a little black lingerie set I didn't recognize. She must have picked it up over the weekend with the girls.

"Come on, Kat, this is an important game," I begged.

"Come on, Kat," she mocked, stalking behind the TV and pulling the power cord from the surge protector. The screen went completely black.

"Seriously?" I exclaimed. I rolled my eyes and took a deep breath, sinking back into the couch. I was so pissed I felt like putting her over my knee and spanking the shit out of her; however, I had a feeling that wouldn't be much of a punishment in her current mood.

Kat

I hadn't seen Evan in a week, and after the sex-crazed week I just had with my girls, I was badly in need of some good dick. He was busy watching basketball, but that was nothing new, and it wasn't every day that we had this beautiful fifteen-room mansion all to ourselves. I had gathered an impressive number of sex toys during my week in Vegas and was excited to put them all to good use. The only problem was I had hardly a clue as to how to use any of them.

After putting my goody bag down next to the couch,

making a dramatic amount of noise in a failed attempt to get Evan's attention, I decided to just stand in front of the TV, knowing that with the sexy new lingerie set Ashley gave us all as a thank-you gift for helping her celebrate, I would grab his attention.

He just leaned around me to keep watching.

What kind of shit is it when you stand in front of your husband half naked after being away for a week and get hardly a response? He had a week of uninterrupted games, and I had more than behaved in Vegas, so I had every right to demand attention. His "Wait one minute, the game is almost over" routine was not going to fly with me tonight, so after a few moments, I took drastic measures and unplugged the TV. There would be plenty of highlights for Evan to watch later, and although I knew it would get on his nerves, I was not going to allow him to put a basketball game over the needs of his horny, aching wife. More often than not, I allowed Evan to get his way, but not this time.

He hollered protest at my latest move, but it didn't take long for him to realize what I was up to in my lingerie.

I crossed to the bag of sex toys I had dropped next to the couch and upended it, depositing all of its contents on the bearskin rug that lay on the floor in front of the couch. I crawled on my hands and knees to sit with it all in front of me, spreading my legs, giving Evan a front seat view of all my goodies. Dildos, paddles, coochie beads, butt plugs, whips, cuffs, nipple clamps, crèmes, blindfolds, a sex book, and a bunch of other items I had never seen before lay on the ground between us. I had one goal in mind for the rest of our stay in this house: Evan was going to show me how to use all of it, and not a room in this place would go unused.

Evan

As Kat sat with her legs splayed in front of me, she showed me more than just the toys she had acquired over the weekend; her brand-new lingerie set came equipped with crotchless panties, and any upset I had about her pulling the plug on the TV vanished.

"You're going to pay for that," I told her, feigning anger.

Her eyebrows shot up; that had been the wrong thing to say to make her believe I was actually mad at her.

"Promise?" she purred, as she spread her legs further apart in front of me and ran her fingers up and down her thigh, leaning back on one elbow.

She fingered through the pages in the sex book, its pages open on the floor for me to peek at from my seat on the couch. I had seen books like that before, and no matter how much the authors advertised them as "X-rated" or "Mind-Blowing," I always found them leaving much to be desired.

"Baby, those books are shit," I blurted out, remnants of bitterness coming out in my words.

She glared at me and pouted as if I had rained on her parade. But then, her adorable pout transformed into a sexy, devilish grin.

"So how about you teach me what this book can't," she suggested, teasingly. "I mean, since you know better, and all."

She leaned forward onto her hands and knees, crawling slowly toward me. As I watched her hips spread out wide behind her and her sexy brown eyes staring directly into mine, I had an idea. I let her crawl all the way toward me and she propped herself up on my lap, kneeling right in front of me. Up close, the delicate details of her black lingerie set became clear. My dick throbbed at the thought of ripping it off of her and fucking her right there on the floor. I pushed those thoughts aside, needing to focus on my plan. Her face was inches in front of mine.

"I promise I will teach you everything I know, and use each and every one of your new toys on you ..." I leaned in closer to her, our lips nearly brushing.

The remote was just behind her on the floor and I hoped to make an attempt at bargaining power. I could still catch the end of the game and then I would be able to focus the rest of the night on my wife. As I moved in closer to her, she leaned backward, not yet knowing what I was plotting.

"I promise I'll fuck you all over this house," I continued, backing her up further. "Right ... after ..."

She was momentarily distracted by my words. Just when I thought I would be successful in grabbing the remote, Kat snapped back into the moment and grabbed the remote from behind her.

"HEY!" Her furrowed brow was more playful than angry. "Not so fast, mister!" She stuck the remote down the front of her bra and ran away, screaming bloody murder. I grabbed a goody off the floor and took off after her, chasing her throughout the house, my final attempt for game-watching an accepted failure.

As mad as I was that I was going to miss the end of the game, I could not be upset for long with my beautiful wife running half-naked through this huge house we had full permission to fuck all over in. With six bedrooms and fifteen rooms total to get freaky in, not including the beautifully renovated basement, I couldn't really complain.

As I chased her around, it was clear I had an advantage over her, as I had spent the day getting familiar with the maze that was this giant house. So it wasn't long before I caught up with her, pinning her down on the floor in the middle of the hallway, her hands above her head.

Knowing my wife, I should have expected her to return from Ashley's bachelorette party fired up and ready to fuck. Although I was sure she learned some things over the week, Kat always looked to me to teach her new sex tricks. I was a few years older than her, and when we first started dating, she was not all that experienced. It turned me on to be her go-to guy, and with seven years of marriage under our belts, I was well aware it was my responsibility as her husband to be ready whenever she was in the mood to learn. She felt safe with me, and because of the confidence I inspired in her, she always trusted to take my lead when it came to new experiences.

With two failed attempts to catch the end of the game, I had to pull all the stops to get back at her. I was going to teach her a thing or two, all right.

As I pinned her hands above her head with one hand, I reached into my pocket with the other, where I had shoved one of the leather gags from Kat's goody bag before running after her. I put the bit in her mouth and fastened the ties behind her head so she couldn't say a word as I fished for details of her weekend.

"So tell me, did you ladies have fun this week?"

A smile attempted to work its way onto Kat's face as she nodded yes, knowing I had given in to her.

"And did you ladies behave this week?"

She smiled even bigger, and shook her head no, clearly teasing me.

"No?" I faked surprise. With one hand securely around her wrists, I grabbed at her ribs, throwing her into a fit of laughter. I didn't stop tickling her until she pleaded through the gag, making all types of indeterminate noises.

"Would you like to take that answer back?"

She nodded violently, desperately wanting the tickling to stop. It didn't look very comfortable to be smiling so hard with her mouth constrained.

"Okay, then." I moved my hand to continue my questioning, letting her breathe a moment.

"Did you guys order strippers this week?"

She nodded slowly.

I caressed one breast and pinched the nipple. "And did they get all the way nude for you ladies?"

Again, she nodded slowly, not knowing where I was headed.

"Did it make your pussy wet, having them dance for you?"

She hesitated before nodding again.

"Seeing them made you want to fuck, didn't it?"

She nodded her head. I could tell my words were having an effect on her.

"You wished I was one of the strippers so you could get fucked right there in front of everyone."

She moved her body underneath me.

"Yes or no?"

She slowly nodded.

Suddenly, I had an idea. Although her sexual appetite was always super high, I didn't need to ask her if she fucked one of the male strippers or not; however, the thought of her in a room with these naked dudes around her had my dick throbbing. There was something so sexy about knowing that even when temptation was most high, her willpower was even higher, and for this simple fact, I wondered if she would allow me to take on this challenge of hers to teach her new things, and if she would have the staying power for what I would surprise her with. I would definitely need help to pull this one off.

"You trust me, right, baby?" I asked.

With eyebrows raised, she slowly nodded.

Kat

Just when I thought Evan was about to fuck me in the middle of the hall, he changed tunes. Of course I trusted him, but the question came so out of the blue it put me on my ass, no pun intended. I had no idea what he was scheming in his head, and I became uneasy. He leaned down and kissed me on the forehead before helping me to my feet.

"Come on, baby," he said calmly.

I was disappointed he didn't take me right then and there, but I suppose if he had to wait to find out who won the game, it was only fair that I wait to get some. He took my hand and led me back to the living room, where he told me to make myself comfortable before he excused himself.

"Stay right here, I'll only be a minute," he told me. "And make sure you keep that gag on, otherwise I'll have to punish you."

I had never been gagged before. My pussy throbbed at the thought of what else Evan had up his sleeve. I assumed my spot on the floor in front of all the toys and took a closer look. I had no idea what some of the items even were, but excitement began to build at the thought of completely submitting myself to Evan as he took me on a sexual adventure this evening.

After his little interrogation in the hallway, it was clear his mind was racing with ideas, and my anticipation had my pussy soaking wet. I grabbed one of the little, pink, lipstick-sized toys I figured was a vibrator and turned it on, pressing it against my clit. Just then, Evan returned, satisfaction playing across his face. I had no idea what he was up to.

As I sat on the floor rubbing my pussy with the vibrator, Evan slowly walked across the room toward me. I leaned back and propped myself up, arching my back and sticking my tits out, my legs spread wide open.

"You said you want me to teach you things that book can't, right, Kat?"

"Mhmm," I moaned, the gag still restricting my ability to speak.

"And you said you trust me, right?"

"Mhmmmm," I moaned again.

He was standing above me now, and as I lay back onto the floor, my pussy ached for him to finally take me. He bent down onto his knees, staring directly into my eyes, his face serious.

"I'm going to need you to do everything I tell you to, no questions asked. Can you do that for me?"

I couldn't speak. I slowly nodded.

He reached between my legs and took the mini vibrator out of my hand. Something pushed against my pussy with slight pressure, followed by vibrations echoing deep inside me. Evan had pushed the vibrator as far as his fingers could reach, and I suddenly felt like I had taken a seat on top of a washing machine.

"Keep that in there," he ordered.

My pussy gushed. I nodded vigorously, bunching my muscles to comply.

"Now I'm going to take the gag out, but I will have to blindfold you. I've enlisted help tonight, and that person should be here soon. If you ever feel the need to stop what's going on around you, all you have to do is say the word 'pineapple.' I promise I'll always be within earshot of you." He took the gag out of my mouth, leaned down and kissed me passionately.

"Remember, just listen for my voice," he told me with a grin.

"Okay," I breathed, as blackness closed in on me, the cool satin tickling my cheeks.

Just then, the doorbell rang ...

Coming Soon by Peekaboo Collins ...

MONOGAMY WITH TREATS

VOL. 2

Connect with me to be notified of new releases,
giveaways, pre-release specials and more:

www.MonogamyWithTreats.com

Instagram: @PeekabooCollins

Twitter: @PeekabooCollins

Facebook: Peekaboo Collins

79664853R00137

Made in the USA
Middletown, DE
11 July 2018